CHRIST: OUR HEALTH

By

DAN LYNCH

© 2002 by Dan Lynch. All rights reserved.

No part of this book may be reproduced, stored in a retrieval system, or transmitted by any means, electronic, mechanical, photocopying, recording, or otherwise, without written permission from the author.

ISBN: 1-4033-4476-0 (e-book)
ISBN: 1-4033-4477-9 (Paperback)

This book is printed on acid free paper.

1stBooks - rev. 09/10/02

CONTENTS

I.	THE BLOOD COVENANT	1
II.	THE RIGHTS AND PRIVILEGES OF THE BELIEVER	7
III.	MANIFESTING HEALTH	20
IV.	HE SENT HIS WORD AND HEALED THEM	30
V.	FAITH AND WHOLENESS	38
VI.	THE DISCIPLINE OF POSITIVE CONFESSION	44
VII.	SPIRITS OF INFIRMITY	55
VIII.	TAKING AUTHORITY	73
IX.	THE CHANNEL: BODY AND SOUL	80
X.	FORGIVENESS: RELEASING THE FLOW	90
XI.	OBEDIENCE	95
XII.	WASHING OF THE BLOOD	104
XIII.	AND THERE WAS LIGHT	117
XIV.	BY HIS STRIPES YE ARE HEALED	123
XV.	WALKING IN THE SPIRIT	132

XVI. PRAISE: GOD'S PRESCRIPTION FOR HEALTH
AND HEALING 139

XVII. CHRIST: OUR HEALTH 151

FORWARD

The believer has been handed the greatest of all jewels as a free gift of grace…the abundant and victorious life in Christ Jesus. We have been blessed… "blessed with every spiritual blessing in heavenly places". The sad truth of the matter is that we still see many believers burdened under the pressures of life…living very unproductive and un-victorious lives. Where is the victory? God reminds us that we are "complete in Him". We have been given *everything* in our salvation! God has withheld nothing. We have it all! His name is Jesus. The frustration of most believers is that they fail to see this "abundance" and "completeness" *manifesting* in their lives. Though we believe we have been blessed it still seems to be still up there in "heavenly places".

Included in our salvation is our *health*. The believer was not 'born again' into the Christ-Life just to remain sick…same as before. Somewhere along the line we have missed the great and wonderful 'mystery' of the abundant life Jesus promised. We have been given the Kingdom yet still walk the dusty paths of the world in carnal living. God has a preferred plan for the health and healing of the believer. Most believers who are sick find themselves in the waiting room at medical clinics and forever standing in prayer lines. The church has all but failed in its teaching our 'completeness' in Christ. We have the *power* within for health and abundant living…but have neglected to *appropriate It*. Christ-in-us is our hope of glory…but we must *release* this great spiritual power we have been given to *experience* its full benefits in the here and now of this life. We must no longer look out to the world hoping for a miracle to pass our way. It is time we begin to mature spiritually and release this dynamic force from within ourselves!

The church has taught and preached the gospel—the Christ of Salvation. Unfortunately, the church has all but neglected to teach the Christ *of Health*. Our salvation is 'complete'…lacking in nothing! We are living under God's New Covenant. This is the Covenant of *perfect* health. God is the God *of perfection!* He did not give us an imperfect Covenant. It is ours!…to know…to claim…to live!

I

THE BLOOD COVENANT

The Cross of Calvary stands at the crossroad of time. Looking back from the cross we see its shadow fall on a cursed people staggering under the weight of sin, sickness, and death...ruled by the Law of God's Old Covenant. The consequence of broken Law exacted very exacting penalties. Man lived in fear...ever under the shadow of death. Looking ahead in time from the cross we see the sunshine of God's grace breaking through all the dark clouds of the Old Covenant. God had written a *New Covenant*...etched indelibly in the heart of man. This was the Blood Covenant of Calvary...the *New Covenant* of love and grace. The thunder stopped, the black clouds rolled away as God smiled down on His creation in loving acceptance of the supreme and final sacrifice of Calvary. Yes, Calvary paid it all. The Blood Covenant of the Cross was a new and living Covenant freeing man from his chains of bondage for all eternity. Jesus had paid the price.

When we receive the lord Jesus into our hearts we are receiving *all* that He died to give us. The moment He comes alive within us we are under the New Covenant of Grace. The shadow of the "Law of death" has been lifted. Jesus died to give us a new Covenant. This new Covenant of Grace contains *everything!* Jesus didn't die to give us an imperfect salvation. The New Covenant is all-inclusive…containing our every need!

Yes, we are *"complete in Him"*. We can still hear His words from the cross to His Father, "it is finished". He completed His earthly task. The book of the Old Covenant Law was closed…sealed by the blood of Jesus. We are now living in the new dispensation of Grace.

God's New Covenant contains *everything*…including *perfect* health! We have been redeemed from the curse of the Law…all the curses of sickness and disease. The New Covenant, God's Blood Covenant, is God's New Testament to His people of *divine health*. We are the redeemed of the Lord…redeemed from all the curses of Deuteronomy 28. The Covenant of Grace is our covenant of *divine health!* We have received the life of Christ activating a new *Law*…the Law of the "Spirit of Life". This new law is a totally new era as the chains of the old law have been broken…and now, "the law of the Spirit of Life in Christ Jesus hath made me free from the law of sin and death." (Rms. 8: 2). Man, up to Calvary, had always been in bondage to the "Law of Sin and Death". Now he is free! The blood of Jesus hath set us free!

Christ: Our Health

From the cross on, the blood of Jesus hath sealed the Covenant of Health to God's children for all eternity. The New Covenant is an eternal Covenant! This Blood Covenant is all-inclusive—lacking in nothing! Our health was paid for at Calvary! "Who his own self bare our sins in his own body on the tree, that we, being dead to sins, should live unto righteousness: by whose stripes ye *were* healed" (I Peter 2: 24). Looking back to the cross God says we "were healed"! If we were healed, we are healed! (Isaiah 53: 5). The New Covenant of Grace contains healing for *every* disease… "Who healeth all thy diseases" (Psm. 103: 3). The New Covenant of Health is ours because Jesus "Himself took our infirmities, and bare our sicknesses" (Math. 8: 17). Jesus took every sickness upon Himself that we might be free to live the victorious life of divine *health!*

Our body is God's *property* (I Cor. 6: 19)…God's *holy temple*. Satan has no *legal right* to God's property! All sickness and disease should be laid at the foot of the cross! We must *not allow* God's property to be defiled! We are the "temple of the Holy Spirit"—filled with praise, filled with honor, and filled with glory. Every atom and cell of our body radiates forth the *Light* of God's Presence. God's property must not be defiled with the sins and contaminations of the world. God's property is *holy*. God's temple radiates the Light of Christ. No dark shadows of disease could possibly exist or survive in the glory Light of God's *Presence*. In the "Law of the Spirit of Life in Christ Jesus" is the ever shining Light of health! It is Jesus' life within that is truly our health.

Divine health is the *divine right* of every blood-bought believer. The New Covenant of health has been sealed by the blood of Jesus. "How much more shall the blood of Christ, who through the eternal Spirit offered himself without spot to God, purge your conscience from dead works to serve the living God? And for this cause he is the mediator of the *new testament*...neither by the blood of goats and calves, but by his *own blood* he entered in once into the holy place, having obtained *eternal redemption* for us…saying, This is the blood *of the testament* which God had enjoined unto you…He *taketh away* the first, that he may establish the *second*. By the which will we are sanctified through the offering of the body of Christ once *for all*...For by one offering he hath *perfected* for ever them that are sanctified." Hebrews 9 and 10 tells of the last and final sacrifice that established the New Covenant. This is God's New Covenant sealed by the blood of Jesus. This was God's seal bringing in an entirely new era for mankind. We are sanctified by the blood, cleansed by the blood, healed by the blood, and perfected by the blood. The blood has been offered upon God's altar in the Heavens, and has washed away the dark shadows of sin's curse and all the plagues of sickness and disease.

God has truly blessed us with *every* spiritual blessing in heavenly places in Christ Jesus. All of God's blessings of grace have been purchased for each of us by the precious blood of Jesus. God's heavenly blessings are *only* claimed by the outstretched hands of faith. It is our faith, and *only our faith*, that transports God's heavenly blessings into the physical realm of manifestation. The New Covenant of Health has already been established and purchased but we can only *experience* it in our *physical* body by *accepting* and *claiming it by faith*. This is all *included* in our salvation!

The church has failed, for the most part, to teach the *all-inclusiveness* of God's New Covenant...allowing the body of Christ to slip back into the many shadows (including sickness) that plague this world. The believer has become so carnally minded that he walks with the world (following all its methods and cures)...*oblivious* to God's New Covenant. It is almost impossible to tell the believer from the unbeliever as far as sickness is concerned. The average Christian seems totally unaware that he has been *redeemed (of all the curses) by the blood of the Lamb. He seems* unaware that his healing was paid for at Calvary. "By whose stripes ye were healed." (I Peter

2:24). The church is sick (like the world) because it has totally overlooked this New Covenant sealed by the blood of Jesus.

Yes, we will continue to be mesmerized by every symptom Satan attempts to attach to our body. He would have us to believe that we are no different than the world (of un-believers). That, alone, should make us mad. Satan's one desire is to keep the believer's mind submerged into the *mindset of the world*...keeping the believer's focus off the Cross and the redemptive work of the Blood. Few of us are even aware of the spiritual warfare being waged by Satan to keep the Cross of the New Covenant obscured and *ineffective* in the lives of believers. The church must *wake up!* The believer must awaken from his materialistic sleep and begin to claim all his rights and privileges of the New Covenant!

We must awaken to our glorious Salvation...a salvation *lacking in nothing!*

II

THE RIGHTS AND PRIVILEGES OF THE BELIEVER

When we are saved, by asking Jesus to come into our hearts as Savior and Lord of our lives, God implants His own Spirit within us…we have become a *new creation* in Christ Jesus. We are now *in-Christ*. We have become a totally new creature…incorporated into the Christ-life. The old life is past away. We have been reborn into a *new life!* Our life has become transported onto a new plane…the *dimension of the Spirit*. Our spiritual senses have been awakened, and we look around and see ourselves living in God's Kingdom of the Spirit. *All things* have become new. Jesus is Lord…and we are seated with Him in heavenly places. We are no longer held in the bondage of law…but are free—living in the realm of Grace. We now find ourselves in a Spiritual World—God's Kingdom of Grace. Yes, we are seated with Jesus in heavenly places…the seat of all power and authority.

How few of us have really grasped the magnitude of our salvation. How few believers really and truly know their rights and privileges in Christ. How few of us realize our total 'completeness in Him'. Yes, Christ has become our life…our hope and glory! Everything is now IN HIM! He is all we will ever need. "In Him we are complete". His life in us is our health, our victory, our everything! "It is no longer I that liveth, but Christ that liveth *in me*". It is time we begin to realize who we are in Christ Jesus…and take hold of all that belongs to us—in Christ. We must begin to redefine our lives in a whole *new identity*. We must begin to live this transposed identity in Christ. If we have received Him into our lives as Lord and Savior then we must allow Him to live His life through us.

All our privileges and rights in Christ are found in God's Word. It is here that He has laid out for us His eternal promises. They are all there in the Word. The sad truth is that we will never possess these promises for ourselves if we do not really know the Word and all that is contained therein…all that is ours in Christ. God has set forth in His Word provisions for our every need. They are all ours to claim. They are all ours to appropriate…if we ever wish to live the victorious life in Christ Jesus. We must find the promises that meet our particular need; we must lift these promises off the printed page; we must personalize these promises by inserting our own name (or the name of the person we are praying for); and we must *speak them forth…ever repeating them with an unrelenting faith until we* see their full manifestation in our lives. "Faith is the *substance* of things hoped for."

"Faith cometh by hearing, and hearing by the word of God". Jesus gave no credit to himself, but told those He healed that it was their own faith that made them *whole*. Yes, it is our *faith in the Word* (above all circumstances and symptoms), as spoken from our lips, that restores our "wholeness".

Jesus is the "Word made flesh". Jesus is the 'living Word'. He plainly tells us that if we 'abide in Him,," and His "Word abides in us" that we will have whatsoever we ask. Jesus said that we must 'drink of His blood, and eat of His flesh'. He is telling us that we must consume all that He is. He must become the very life of our life. We must bring Jesus, the LIVING WORD, into the flesh of our flesh: in spirit, soul, mind, and body. This is the secret. This is God's great mystery. Yes, we have it all. His name is Jesus!

In the New Covenant we have been "blessed with *every* spiritual blessing in Christ", yet fail to see it manifesting, experientially, in our lives. The secret of manifestation is found in the art of *appropriation*. It is all ours in Christ…but we must appropriate it! Our victory and our health are *in* Christ through His infallible Word…but we must appropriate it. We must appropriate it to the totality of our lives…to our minds, to our bodies, to our circumstances, to our finances—to everything we need to live the abundant and victorious life. It is true we live under Grace...but God's grace must be activated by our faith and specifically appropriated by our lips to meet our needs. "In Him we are complete" ...but our 'completeness' can only manifest as we *live in Him* and His *Words abide in us*...through the manifesting process of appropriations. The church, for the most part, has never really taught the *laws of manifestation* and the *art of appropriation.* Though we have been given it all in Christ our lives seem empty and unfulfilled...never truly realizing the abundant life Jesus promised.

The New Covenant is the Covenant of Faith. We receive everything Jesus died to give us through faith. Faith is developed through knowing *personally* God's Word and is activated by our *speaking* God's Word. The scriptures are God's love letters to us...filled with all His promises. To manifest our health we must search out all the scriptural promises of health and healing. When we establish these in our heart they become the foundation of our health and healing. "He sent his WORD, and healed them" (Psm. 107: 20). Take to heart these healing scriptures. They are your rights and privileges as established in the New Covenant. They are all yours *if* you know them in your heart, personalize them, claim them as your own, and appropriate them through *daily* affirmation. There are many, many healing scriptures that can build your faith. Here are a few of the foundation ones compiled here for your convenience:

HEALTH AND HEALING SCRIPTURES

"For I will restore HEALTH unto thee, and I will HEAL thee of thy wounds, saith the Lord"

Jer. 30: 17

"Himself took our infirmities, and bare our sicknesses"

Math. 8: 17

"Surely He hath BORNE our griefs, and carried our sorrows: Yet we did esteem him stricken, smitten of God, and afflicted. But He was wounded for our' transgressions, He was bruised for our iniquities: the chastisement of our peace was UPON HIM; AND WITH HIS STRIPES WE ARE HEALED"

Isaiah 53: 4, 5

"and ye shall serve the Lord your God, and he shall bless thy bread, and thy water; and I will take SICKNESS AWAY FROM THE MIDST OF THEE"

Exodus 23: 25

"And the Lord will TAKE AWAY FROM THEE ALL SICKNESS, and will put none of the EVIL DISEASE of Egypt, which thou knowest, upon thee"

Deut. 7: 15

"Bless the Lord, O my soul: and all that is within me bless his holy name. Bless the Lord O my soul, and forget not all his benefits: who forgiveth all thine iniquities; who HEALETH ALL thy DISEASES; who REDEEMETH thy life from destruction: who crowneth thee with loving kindness and tender mercies, who satisfieth thy mouth with good things; so that thy YOUTH is RENEWED like the eagles"

Psm. 103: 1-5

"And they laid the sick in the streets, and besought him that they might touch if it were but the border of his garment: and as many as TOUCHED HIM were made WHOLE"

Mark 6: 56

"There shall NO EVIL befall thee, neither shall ANY PLAGUE come nigh thy dwelling. For he shall give his ANGELS charge over thee, to keep thee in all thy ways"

Psm. 91:10, 11

"Know ye not that your BODIES are MEMBERS OF CHRIST?"

I Cor. 6: 15

"there is but one God, the Father, OF WHOM ARE ALL THINGS, and we IN HIM; and one Lord, Jesus Christ, BY WHOM ARE ALL THINGS, and we BY HIM"

I Cor. 8: 6

"The law of the SPIRIT OF LIFE in Christ Jesus hath made me FREE from the law of SIN AND DEATH"

Rms. 8: 2

"Know ye not that your BODY is the TEMPLE of the HOLY Ghost which is IN you, which ye have of God, and ye are NOT YOUR OWN? For ye are bought with a price: therefore glorify God in your BODY, and in your spirit, which are God's"

I Cor. 6:19, 20

"That the LIFE also of Jesus might be made MANIFEST in our body…that the life also of Jesus might be made MANIFEST in our MORTAL FLESH"

II Cor. 4: 10, 11

"Therefore if any man be IN CHRIST, he is a NEW CREATURE: old things are *passed away*; behold, ALL THINGS are become NEW"

II Cor. 5: 17

"That was the true LIGHT, which *lighteth every man that cometh into the world*"

John 1: 9

"Then shall thy LIGHT break forth as the morning, and thine HEALTH shall *spring forth speedily*: and the RIGHTEOUSNESS shall go before thee; and the glory of the Lord shall be thy reward"

Isa. 58: 8

"Behold, I give unto you power to tread on serpents and scorpions, and *over all the power of the enemy*: and *nothing* shall by any means hurt you"

Luke 10: 19

"For God hath not given us the spirit of fear; but of power, and of love, and of a sound mind"

II Tim. 1: 7

"Stand perfect, and complete in all the Will of God"

Col. 4:12

"Put on the NEW MAN, which after God is created in righteousness and true *holiness*"

Eph. 4: 24

"For ye were sometimes darkness, but now are ye Light in the Lord: walk as *children of Light*"

Eph. 5: 8

"it is God which *worketh in you* both to will and to do of His good pleasure"

Phil. 2: 13

"Christ *in you,,the* hope of Glory"

Col. 1-27

"For *in* Him dwelleth all *the fulness* of the Godhead bodily. Ye are COMPLETE IN HIM"

Col. 2: 9, 10

"Until Christ be FORMED IN YOU"

Gal. 4: 19

"Christ bath REDEEMED us from the curse of the Law"

Gal. 3: 13

"SPEAK THE WORD ONLY, and my servant shall be HEALED"

Math. 8-8

"Go thy way; and as thou hast BELIEVED, so be it DONE UNTO THEE"

Math. 8: 13

"Daughter, thy FAITH hath MADE THEE WHOLE"

Math. 8: 13

"Who his own self bare our sins in his own body on the tree, that we, being dead to sins, should live unto RIGHTEOUSNESS: BY WHOSE STRIPES YE *WERE* HEALED"

I Peter 2: 24

"And they OVERCAME him by the BLOOD OF THE LAMB, and by the WORD OF THEIR TESTIMONY"

Rev. 12: 11

"For the WORD OF GOD is quick, and powerful; and sharper than any two-edged sword, piercing even to the dividing asunder of soul and spirit, and of the joints and marrow"

Heb. 4: 12

"Hold fast the faithful WORD"

"The WORD OF GOD, which *effectually* worketh also *in you* that believe"

I Thes. 2: 13

"And ye shall know the TRUTH, and the Truth shall make you free"

John 8: 32

Sin shall not have dominion over you: for ye are not under the law, but under Grace"

Rms. 6: 19

"And we know that all *things* work together for *good* to them that love God"

Rms. 8: 28

"Have faith in God. For verily I say unto you, that whosoever shall SAY unto this mountain, BE THOU REMOVED, and be thou cast into the sea; and shall NOT DOUBT in his heart, but shall BELIEVE that those things which he saith shall come to pass; he shall HAVE *whatsoever he saith*"

Mark 11: 23

"Christ shall be MAGNIFIED in my *body*"

Phil. 1: 20

"Christ IS ALL and IN ALL"

Col. 3: 11

"Beloved, I wish above all things that thou mayest prosper and be in HEALTH, even as thy *soul* prospereth"

III John 2

This is *your* Covenant. Claim it!

How much more our rights and privileges in Christ come into focus when we understand God's Word, His Covenant, and the *spiritual* nature of all life…God's all-inclusive Presence. God has a *preferred plan* for the health and healing of the believer! Something we have totally overlooked. Still we look for healing from without…and have ignored the inner reality of God's Presence. God's Presence of Light only manifests health! God's Presence within waits patiently to release itself into the physical manifestations of health. We have been so mesmerized to outer delusions that we have failed to see God's glorious Kingdom of Light within…an inward spiritual force waiting to be released.

When we became born-again our body became the temple of the Holy Spirit. The Spirit of God came to take up residence in this, God's holy sanctuary. How easy it is to abandon our commitment and responsibility to this dynamic force within and allow ourselves to be controlled by the outside world…just like we did before we were saved. This inward force can only be released through the dedicated commitment to spiritual growth and spiritual living. The average Christian has not progressed past the first rudiments of salvation…and has failed to vision the infinite dimensions of God's Kingdom within. Jesus said: "The Kingdom of God is within you". How lax and complacent we have become in allowing ourselves to fall back into the mind-set and routines of the world.

The world can little distinguish the believer from the un-believer…both entangled in worldly living. How little spiritual Light emanates from the soul of most believers. The victorious life will only begin to be lived and experienced when we come into the realization as to who *we are in Christ*…and *all that we have* in His awesome and all-inclusive Life. Let us now take hold of all our privileges of Grace and begin to live the victorious life in Christ Jesus!

III

MANIFESTING HEALTH

"Whatsoever doth make manifest is Light"

Eph. 5: 13

Light is the foundation of all manifest creation. God ignited the process of manifestation with His resounding words—"Let there be Light". Light was the formalization of God's eternal Spirit in its progression to the cellular plane of Effect. The great Light vibration became the very fabric of this atomic universe. The essence of all physical appearance is the atomic vibration of Light…giving rise to the molecular vibration…giving rise to the cellular vibration…giving form, shape, and color to this 'material' plane of Effect. Cause and Effect. Life, as we know and experience it, is the plane of sense perception. The Spirit of God moved, through the vehicle of Light, to its myriad formations on this sensory plane of effects. The *reality* of all life is God's *Omnipresent Spirit!* God's Omnipresence is endowed with His omniscience (all-knowing), and His Omnipotence (all-power). The reality of this unseen, atomic reality in which we live is composed of God's Omnipresence Omniscience, and, Omnipotence…flashing as form, through our senses, on the screen of consciousness. It is fundamental that we understand the spiritual reality of our universe (our bodies included) to truly understand manifesting health. God originally composed our body in His spiritual "image and likeness". This body was perfect in every detail…of flawless design. This was an eternal body…sinless, sickless, and deathless. Only by sin came death. The consequence of sin led to the diseases and the breakdown of God's holy creation…a body severed from its spiritual source. The consequence of sin's separation was death. Sickness and the demons of disease had never even entered the picture. God's originally created body was holy…radiating the Light of perfect health. God's Omnipresence was the spiritual structure of Adam's perfect body. Health was synonymous to the holiness of God's spirit essence formalizing the human body in His image and likeness.

The human body is the most complex mechanism ever created. How every body part and organ functions in perfect unison can only be a testimony to the miracle working power of God's indwelling Omniscience. Without this the body would cease to function in a moment's time. To view the simplicity of God's Presence we should not get too entangled in a medical web of medical terminology. We must view the body in the simplicity of its atomic structure of atoms and cells…knowing that God's Omnipresent Spirit is the reality and substance of every cell. The reality of every cell is God's Omnipresence, the function of every cell is God's Omniscience, and the life-forces of every cell is God's Omnipotence.

Scripture tells us that we are God's workmanship...His property. "Know ye not that your body is the Temple of the Holy Ghost which is in you, which ye have of God, and ye are not your own? For ye are bought with a price: therefore glorify God in your body, and in your Spirit, which are God's," (1 Cor. 6: 19, 20). Have we really considered our body, with all its miracle workings of complex intra-structure, as God's *holy* Temple? The reverence of this concept alone would cause much disease to totally evaporate. Our body is *God's property*...and can only truly function in the spiritual light of pure holiness. "Put on the new man, which after God is created in righteousness and true holiness" (Eph. 4: 24).

Have we ever really considered the *spiritual* reality and make up of our body, God's Temple? Have we really considered the life and substance of the cell composed of God's Omnipresence, Omniscience, and Omnipotence? Yes, we are Spirit beings, possessing a soul, and living in a body. Even the atomic, cell composition of the body is composes of God's all-inclusive Spirit. "Ye also, as lively stones, are built up a *spiritual house*"

Christ: Our Health

(I Peter 2: 5). Every cell is a "lively stone" structuring our body of pure Spirit. "There is but one God, the Father, *of whom are all things*, and we *in Him*" (I Cor. 8: 6). God is the invisible spiritual Reality...the sum and substance of all manifest creation.

Jesus is coming back for His bride...a glorious church...without "spot or wrinkle"—a church "holy and without blemish" (Eph. 5: 27). In these 'last days' before Christ's return there will be a *purifying* of the body of Christ. Jesus is returning to establish His millennium Kingdom. He is returning for a glorious and victorious church. This can only mean a well church! He is not coming back for a sickly bride.

We have been taught the Christ of Salvation, but not the Christ of Health. Jesus said that we are *"complete* in Him" (Col. 2-10). This means our Salvation is all-inclusive containing everything we will ever need in this life. The most important thing is being saved, of course, but the church has, somehow, overlooked the total picture of "completeness" in our salvation...the 'abundant life' in the here *and now* that Jesus promised. Jesus is our salvation...for He *is* Life eternal. But, Jesus is, also, our healer...our health; Jesus is our provider...our provision; Jesus is our protector...our protection; Jesus is out victory, our wisdom, our Love, our peace, our strength, our everything! Let us not forget the *Christ of Health! His life, within* us, can *only* be pure, radiant HEALTH!! We have been taught the Christ of Salvation, but not the *Christ of Health!* If, throughout all the years, we had been taught the Christ of Health, as we had been taught the saving Christ we would have built up within us the same faith for our *healing* as for our salvation!

God can certainly look down and decree miracle health for His children (as He did for Israel leaving Egyptian slavery) or, more than likely, He will allow our faith to build up (through teaching of the Word) in the area of health…so the church can, overcome the demons of sickness and disease. It will be unto us according to our *faith!* How important, in these last days, to get our faith built to the degree that it will begin to *release from within* the forces of healing and health! Yes, Christ is returning for a radiantly well church…a church without spot or wrinkle! For the most part, the healing of the believer will be the *process* of manifestation.

God "sent His Word and healed them" (Psm. 107:20).

God heals through His Word. We must know the Word…*every* healing scripture we can find! Even though we have been living under God's Covenant of Health all these years, we have had no real teaching in this area to *build up* our faith...and it is our *"faith that makes us whole"*.

How do we manifest health for our own bodies? First, we must see our body as God's *property*...the Temple of the Holy Spirit. Second, we must come to know the indwelling presence of the Holy Spirit as our friend and constant *companion*. Third, we must see our body as spiritual...made of the atomic structure of pure Light. Fourth, we must know, without a doubt, that we have, within ourselves, all the *life forces* of health *waiting to be Released*. Fifth, we must see our spirit, soul, mind, and body bound in the unity of holiness...a purity transcending all the sins and contaminations of the world. Sixth, we must always 'walk in the Spirit'...embracing the spiritual quality of divine health every minute. Seventh, we must praise the God of Creation...ever singing forth the praises of God's *New Covenant*: the CHRIST OF HEALTH!

Our health is *in Christ*, and must be released from within. Yes, we must consciously release *resurrection power* from the center of every cell to the 'quickening' vibration of health and healing. Once healing is established then we must discipline ourselves in *spiritual living* to maintain a life-style of health. Our health will be maintained in proportion to the amount of light emanating from each cell. This Light-Source will be maintained in proportion to the degree of holiness pervading all the areas of spirit, soul, mind, and body. Holiness is necessary for the *spiritual transparency* necessary to transmit Light! Holiness maintains our unity with God…and God is Light, and in Him is no darkness.

Yes, our health will be in proportion to the degree of holiness establishing the purity of the cell life. Every cell has a life of its own…a world in itself. Every cell is the miracle manifestation of God's love. Every cell is a 'living consciousness' that must be purified and sanctified by the blood of Jesus…cleansed of all worldly contaminations…free from the disease of sin.

Have we ever considered the 'world of the cell'? Every cell is an entity unto itself with its own consciousness and inherent intelligence. This is not the 'thinking' intelligence we associate with the mind, but, rather, the inherent omniscience of God's wisdom controlling the creative processes of all life. Because of this, sin can so saturate the consciousness of man's mind that it can eventually filter down into the consciousness of the cell-life—inhibiting its normal function. This is the true source of all disease…the inharmony of sin and a life out of tune to the creative flow of life.

The mind is the 'housekeeper' of the body and must be pure and sin-free if it is to ever maintain the natural purity inherent in the cell life. It is so important to keep a guard stationed at the entrance of the mind…ever guarding it against sinful and worldly thoughts that would contaminate it in anyway. The thought-life of the mind must always be tuned to God's Word. God's Word is the compass of the mind. It keeps us walking the 'straight and narrow'…ever resisting all the 'pulls' from the world of darkness and sensuality. We must always keep our consciousness in *harmony* to God's eternal Word of Creation. God's Word is the ongoing act of creation. Yes, God not only created the world of matter with His Word, but creation itself is an ongoing process ever *responding* to God's resounding Words of Life! The dis-ease of the cell-life is simply the discords of a life out of tune to God's eternal Word. Creation is an onflowing river that cannot be dammed up in anyway.

The divine health inherent in the structure of the cell must be released from within. As born-again Christians we have the power of the Holy Spirit resident within. This is a power that must be recognized and released if we wish to see divine health manifesting consistently. The spiritual quality of divine health manifests as power is released. Jesus said, "The Kingdom of God is *within* you". The spiritual nature of true health is only found within. If we are seeking outside sources for our health we are looking in the wrong places. God's Kingdom is within! Let us thank God for the creative power we have within ourselves in the person of the Holy Spirit. It is God's Word that builds our faith, and it is our faith that releases Holy Ghost power!

Let us live every moment in an attitude of worship, ever praising the God of creation, that the life of Christ within will ever be radiating the light of holiness. Holiness *is* health! Jesus' life within is the totality of our being. His life expressing *is* our health! It is altogether pure. It is His life that radiates the light of health from the center of every cell. Let this be our constant prayer affirmation in the maintenance of perfect health:

"Thank you, Father, that the resurrection power of the Holy Spirit is now being released from the center of every cell of my body-temple radiating forth the Light of your indwelling Presence".

Amen

Maintaining health does not happen by itself. It is a work. It is a conscious discipline. God operates His universe by exacting principles. It is our responsibility to know these principles found in His Word, and apply them to every area of our life: spirit, soul, mind, and body. The life-style of maintaining health in full manifestation is an inner discipline…keeping our body fine-tuned to the harmonious flow of God's creative life.

IV

HE SENT HIS WORD AND HEALED THEM

"Let the word of Christ *dwell in you* richly."

(Col. 3:16)

"Speak the word *only*."

(Math. 8:8)

"*Holding fast* the faithful word."

(Titus 1:9)

"*Upholding all things* by the word of his *power*."

(Heb. 1:3)

"Receive with meekness the *engrafted* word"

(Jam. 1:21)

"They *overcame* him by the blood of the lamb, and by the *word* of their testimony"

(Rev. 12:11)

"Every word of God is *pure*"

(Prov. 30:5)

"The word of our God shall *stand forever*"

(Isaiah 40:8)

"Man shall not live by bread alone, but by *every* word of God"

(Luke 4:4)

"The seed is the word of God."

(Luke 8:11)

"*Blessed* are they that hear the word of God, and *keep it*."

(Luke 8:11)

"*Faith* cometh by *hearing*, and hearing by the word of God"

(Rom. 10:17)

"to fulfill the word of God"

(Col. 1:25)

"the word of God, which *effectively worketh* also *in you* that believe"

(I Thes. 2:13)

"The word of God is quick and *powerful*"

(Heb. 4:12)

"the word of *God abideth in you*"

(I John 2:14)

"In the beginning was the Word…and the *Word was God*"

(John 1:1)

"thou shalt see now whether *my word* shall come *to pass* unto thee…"

(Num. 11:23)

"I will hasten my word to *perform it*"

(Jer. 1:12)

"*if* thou wilt walk in my statutes…then will *I perform my word* with thee…"

(I Kings 6:12)

"So shall my *word* be that *goeth* forth out of my mouth; it shall *not return unto me void*, but it shall *accomplish* that which I please, and it shall *prosper* in the *thing whereto I sent* it."

(Isaiah 55:11)

Behold the *living* word! These are spirit words and creative in nature. God created the worlds with his spoken word: "And God said, let there be…" Once we grasp the revelation of the *inherent power* in God's words we can speak forth the word of God with complete faith for it to *accomplish* whereto it is sent. These are not ordinary words. These are powerful, living, and creative words. The scriptures are full of, "thus saith the Lord." God speaks-and *miracles* happen! Everything God spoke he did—and everything he did was *a miracle!* God lives in the world of the *supernatural*. How our finite senses limit our perception of God—we see through the "glass darkly" of our dulled senses. God give us spiritual ears and spiritual eyes that we might behold your presence ever surrounding us and behold your hand ever moving! God is on the throne, high and lifted up, ever watching the affairs of man. His voice resounds through the heavens. God, give us ears to hear. Let us ride on the tide of your eternal words and watch the wonders of their creation. He upholds all things by his *living words!* Creation is a continuous, on-going drama responding to God's resounding words! But could we grasp these words and put them to work in our lives—making Jesus a *reality* within us. Once we catch hold of the significance and magnitude of God's words victorious living will be within our reach!'

Our salvation not only includes eternal life but *everything* we need down here to live the abundant and victorious life! As we learn to appropriate the power of the Holy Spirit through God's *living words* we will begin to know in experience all that salvation includes. God's Word contains promises that encompass the entire spectrum of salvation. Our lives must echo these words of promise for us to come into the complete realization of the meaning of salvation—the abundant life in Christ Jesus. God promises to all his children in Christ the abundant life—a life of health for by "Jesus stripes ye are healed"; a life *victorious* for "ye are more than conquerors in Christ Jesus"; a life of *protection* for he has "given his angels charge over thee"; a life of *security* for "my God supplies all my needs according to his riches in glory by Christ Jesus"; a life of *blessings* for "God hath blessed us with every spiritual blessing in heavenly places in Christ Jesus". God's Word is truth. God's Word is faithful. He will never go back on his Word. He will move mountains, if necessary, to *fulfill His* Word! Let us take hold of these "living words" of God that these promises might be ours!

God's words are the switch for turning on the power. The Holy Spirit is the power for fulfillment, but the Spirit is propelled to its objective by the *spoken* word. God says to believe and speak forth His Word with all boldness. He will see to it that His Word (God's will in action) will accomplish that to which it is sent. We must appropriate the Spirit as if it were a giant laser beam, by activating it with our *faith* and targeting it by our words. Let your words send forth a steady stream of light until this 'spiritual laser' has brought about the manifest result. Let this holy light be beamed into every diseased cell until healing and health is totally restored! Hallelujah! "God sent His Word and healed them!" Let us raise our vision that we might see into the spiritual realm and see these promises as *realities!* Let us see and take hold of the living Word. Let us see the spiritual nature of this world. Let us see the spiritual nature of our own lives—even our bodies! If we could see the atomic reality of our physical body as *pure light* in the spiritual realm, the Word would have an easy time of it in its mission of restoration. God give us a spiritual vision to behold a *spiritual world!*

Jesus described himself—the "Word"—as a living seed that needed to be planted in good soil to produce fruit for the kingdom. The more we project God's living words into the soil of our subconscious, the more likely it will be firmly planted. As we lovingly care for this implanted Word within us the more likely it will germinate and become fruitful in our lives. The *implanted* Word! The good soil is the ground of our subconscious that has the 'God kind of faith' to produce a rich harvest. The seed must continually be cared for and watered—never uprooted by doubt. We must never allow Satan entrance to dig up our garden—we must care for it and protectively watch over our words that we not nullify its growth by negative confessions. We must live by faith and not by sight. Therefore, we must side with *God's word* regardless of circumstances, symptoms, and physical evidence. We must stand by the Word at all costs! We must never negate the Word by speaking words that do not line up with God's words. With faith and patience—in God's time—we will see the fruits of God's implanted words in our lives. To activate and germinate these seed-words they must be planted so deep that they actually enter into the spirit-realm. The realm of the *Spirit* is the realm of the miraculous! The more these spirit-words are spoken forth the deeper they are planted. Affirm the word continuously, boldly, courageously—without wavering—and you will see them transformed into tangible realities. Like the metamorphosis of the butterfly taking wings so will your words be changed—by the power of the Holy Spirit—into *physical manifestation*.

Yes, words are 'creative'. Guard your words because you will <u>get what you say</u>. Be careful not to say discouraging, negative, or harmful words—as they will come back to you riding the waves. Words can destroy. Make sure you know your Bible that you speak forth *only* God's words: "Thou shalt also decree a thing, and it shall be *established* unto thee." (Job. 22:28)

Let your living, Godly words propel your faith so that the Spirit of power will hit its mark every time. Let us live in the power of the "Living Word" and see the *Christ-in-us* grow into the abundant, victorious life we have been promised. There is *power* in the *spoken word* to give form and meaning to our world. Our words produce direction and purpose to life. Let us learn the management of words that they might be productive and fruitful. Let our creative words speak forth *creative lives!*

Let us say with Mary, "Be it unto me according to thy Word."

V

FAITH AND WHOLENESS

"Thy Faith hath made thee whole"

Math. 8: 13

With these few words Jesus gave us the formula for healing and health. Everything we receive from God is by the outstretched hands of faith. God is a God of Faith. Without faith we could never comprehend the reality of the invisible God. Jesus tells us that it is our faith, and only our faith, that will make us "whole". Health *is* our wholeness! Healing is the manifesting process restoring God's *original pattern of wholeness.*

What is wholeness? Wholeness is, simply, the unity of man's three part being: spirit, soul, and body...embraced in spiritual oneness. God's all-encompassing Spirit must shine through man's soul to the engulfing of his body-temple in the Light of pure holiness. God is Light...and in Him is no darkness whatsoever. All sickness and disease is bred in sin's swamps of darkness...the breeding ground of all germs spawning every disease imaginable. God is altogether holy. No sin or demon of disease could possibly survive, or even enter, the Light of God's holiness. Holiness is wholeness.

Have we ever equated *holiness* with health? In considering such a question the first thing our minds turn to is remembering friends, relatives, and many good Christians that died before their time of some dreadful disease. But, does this make God's Word any less true? God says that He "wishes above all things that we be in health and prosper, just as our souls prosper" (111 John 2). God says that because of "Jesus' stripes we are healed" (Isaiah 53: 5). God says that "Jesus took our infirmities, and bare our sicknesses" (Math.8: 17). God says "Christ bath redeemed us from the curse of the Law', (Gal. 3: 13). Yes, we have been redeemed from the *curse of sickness* by the precious blood of Jesus. We are living under the New Covenant sealed by the blood of Jesus. We have been taught the Saving Jesus, but have little teaching when it comes to the Healing Jesus. We have been taught to look up to Jesus in our prayers for healing, but have not come into the full realization of Christ, in *all His health*, living on the *inside of us*. We have not been taught the *principles of faith for healing* and the appropriation of the Word to the cells of our body. Yes, many wonderful Christians were never shown the Christ of Health, and never were taught the healing scriptures, and never realized that healing and health is the *releasing* of God's healing power from *within*. The church failed them. The church must now wake up and begin to teach the *realities of God's Kingdom!* In these last days God is closing the door on creeds, ceremonies, traditions, and just plain ignorance of His Word. We are just about to enter the Millennium age. Jesus is coming back for a healthy, victorious, and glorious church!

Exactly what is faith? Scripture tells us that faith is a "substance"—the tangible substance of things hoped for. It is man's 'sixth sense' enabling him to *believe* in the reality of the invisible God...the Creator and Source of all life. How do we obtain faith? God has given each of us a "measure of faith". It is built in. God, nevertheless, expects us to take this faith, plant it, water it, and cause it to grow into *great* faith. How do we do this? Scripture tells us that "faith cometh by *hearing*, and hearing by the Word of God" (Rms. 10:17). Jesus said that God's Word is like a little seed, but, if we plant it deep in our spirit, it will begin to *grow* and bear much fruit in our lives. We must study and meditate on God's eternal Word that the Word will actually become "flesh" of our bodily flesh and begin to produce living realities within us. The Word will produce the fruits of health, when healing scriptures are deeply planted in our spirit. We must search out, memorize, personalize, and *speak-forth* God's holy Word over our lives!

We must blanket our lives with the Word and let it totally saturate our spirit, our soul, our mind, and our body. Yes, faith, through God's living Word, is truly the "evidence of things not seen". Our faith comes by our hearing (as we speak forth God's Word with all boldness). Behold, the *implanted* Word, which effectually works in the lives of all who believe. It is alive and growing…as long as we water it with loving care *daily* speaking, daily decreeing God's living Words over our lives. Faith is the *power of manifestation.* It is the living Word of our faith, activating the inner power of the Holy Spirit, that manifests our wholeness…our health.

Again, what is wholeness? Wholeness is the *spiritual unity* of our three-part man…the alignment of spirit, soul, and body in perfect order. *Every thought* of our mind must be aligned in perfect order to God's Word. *Every feeling* of our soul must be aligned to and ever expressing God's Love life. *Every* cell of our body must be aligned in perfect health through the indwelling power of the Holy Spirit. Wholeness is the *entirety* of our being *incorporated in the Christ-life.* Wholeness is our health.

The life of health is lived *in Christ.* As Christians we have the life of Christ within us in the person of the Holy Spirit…and it is our responsibility to keep this life manifesting in all its glory and health! This is a whole new dimension of living. Our wholeness of health can never be separated from our *quality of life*. Yes, there is a dimension to life, and a dimension to health we have never dreamed of!

God's New Covenant of Health is sealed *by* the Spirit, lived *in* the Spirit, and manifested *through* the Spirit. If we are to realize this Covenant, experientially, then we must agree to all the terms of the contract. It does not just happen. We have our responsibilities if this contract of health is to be honored. The New Covenant, written in the blood of Jesus, is a Covenant of holiness and absolute purity. This is our responsibility. Men of the Old Testament, separated from God's Life-source, never had the power within to live up to God's Commandments (the Law) of purity and holiness. But, thank God, we now have the *power!* The blood of Jesus has written a New Covenant. The blood of Jesus has given us new life. The blood of Jesus has endowed us with the inner *power* of the *Holy Spirit*. The Blood has set us free! We now have the *power!* Yes, we now have, within ourselves, Holy Spirit power to help us live a life of purity. The Holy Spirit is within each spirit-filled believer waiting to be *released!* Our responsibility is to realize and experience the *purity of health* through the *power* of the *Holy Spirit*. Our health is *already* established in the Blood Covenant, but it is our responsibility to release it into full manifestation! The full manifestation of our health is found in our wholeness and union to the living Christ we now have, as born-again believers, living on the inside. We are now *in Christ!* Our whole identity must be dissolved into the Light of the living Christ within us. Our *new identity* must be *Christ*...Christ alone! It is no longer 'I' that liveth, but *Christ* that liveth *in me* (Gal-2: 20). We must come into the total realization of Christ as our life...our wholeness...our health. When the Word of Faith comes alive on the inside of us it activates the life of Christ as a *living reality* within us. This life can only be activated through our faith of inner recognition. Our faith must release the *healing power* of the Christ within. There can be *no sickness* in the *living Christ!!* Our health will manifest in proportion to our realization of this *new identity*. This is not simply an intellectual knowing. This is our entire being submerged and dissolving into the *Christ-life*. This is a purity and transparency of consciousness revealing Christ living on the inside of us.

Our health is *in Christ*. Let us moment by moment release our faith...and realize our wholeness in Christ.

VI

THE DISCIPLINE OF POSITIVE CONFESSION

"Death and Life are in the power of the tongue"

Prov. 18: 21

"My son, *attend to my words*, incline thine ear unto my sayings. Let them not depart from thine eyes; *keep them* in the *midst of thine heart*. For they are life unto those that find them, and *health* to all their flesh"

Prov. 4: 20-22

James writes in his epistle, "If any man *offend not* in *word*, the same is a *perfect man*" (James 3: 2). Words have the power to *create*! He says that words are to our lives like a bit in a horse's mouth or the small rudder of a large ship. They can turn our lives in most any direction. They have the power to create…or destroy. They can even determine our eternal destiny! How important it is that we learn the discipline of the *management of words*.

We live in a self-centered 'getting' society. Our world is one of self-gratification. How easy it is to become despondent and discouraged when we don't 'get' what we want…and find negative confessions coming out of our mouth before we even realize it. Yes, we must learn the discipline of *guarding our thoughts* and *managing our words*. We will *get* what we *say!* Words are creative…whether they be on the positive or negative side of the ledger. James goes on to say that the tongue can be a "fire" that is capable of defiling and destroying the whole body. He says that the tongue can be an "unruly evil, full of deadly poison", and that from the same mouth can proceed blessing and cursing. He goes on to say that a fountain should not usher forth both sweet and bitter water. It is a wise man that orders his conversation aright…bringing forth only the sweet waters. A wise man will show out of a "*good* conversation his works with meekness of wisdom".

We, as Christians, have it in our hearts to order the words of our mouth with the good, the kind, and the lovely. We try our best to make good, positive confessions. But, how often we nullify our confessions in *unguarded* moments as we go about our busy lives in day-to-day living. How easy it is for our frustrations and irritations to come bubbling to the surface…and out our mouth…completely canceling all our good confessions! We confess health, but, in an unguarded moment unwittingly confess "I believe I'm coming down with a cold" …completely succumbing to symptoms, and the mindset of the world. We confess prosperity, but, in an-other unguarded moment, throw up our hands in frustration that we can't pay the bills... "I just can not ever seem to get out of debt—" How easy it is for our subconscious (and our unruly tongue) to dig holes that we can't seem to get out of! How easy it is, for even good Christians, to allow the fears, anxieties, frustrations, and hate of the world to invade their subconscious. Everything in this deep mind within seems to, eventually, rise up to the surface and find release through our words.

We must learn to place a guard at the gates of our mind! God's holy Word is the only reliable guard...a guard that wont fall asleep. Our mind can only really be protected with the Truth. God's Word is Truth. Yes, it is the "Truth" that *sets us* free! Even though we have read the scriptures the Word can easily be overpowered by the voices of the world bombarding us from all directions. The Word must be *daily read and confessed. The Word must be given the offensive posture of warfare! We are in spiritual warfare*, whether we know it or not! The Word must be read, meditated, digested, and devoured if it is really to become submerged in our sub-conscious to the point of overcoming all the preset negatives in these lower regions. The Word is our *armor* of protection...ever protecting our mind. The Word is our sword...our offensive weapon of battle.

Christ: Our Health

Once we *consciously* have the Word on "guard", stationed at the gates of our mind ever watchful for unconscious reactions and responses, then we must discipline our mouth to *only* positive confession. If we wish to live a life of health, victory, and abundance then this discipline is a must! If we have never set personal goals and objectives for our lives then our words can also reflect little meaning. We must first know what we want and desire to come to pass! We must focus our lives. We will never be able to put *words to our desires if we don't know clearly* what we really want out of this life. If we want health then we must *always* have a picture of health in our mind's eye. With all the world's methods of medicine, and all the television commercials (selling every 'cure' imaginable) it is no wonder we are sickly and yielding to every symptom Satan would attach to our body! Do we really have a *clear picture* of our body as God's property...His *holy* temple...filled with the *power* of the Holy Spirit? Do we have a clear picture that we are not OF this world (with all its plagues and sickness) but, as Christians, are now *in Christ?* Do we really see ourselves as the REDEEMED...redeemed from the curse of sickness...living under God's NEW COVENANT of health? Do we have the beautiful picture in our mind of 'Christ being magnified in our body'? (Phil. 1: 20)

We will never truly be able to express in words what we desire if we do not have a *clear picture* of who we are *in* Christ. Our words are powerful and creative, but can only express our deep convictions. How many of us can honestly say we have deep convictions and unwavering desires? Every successful man or woman has real goals, convictions, and desires that wont give up. These are ingredients all successful people put to work for their success in business. Why don't we put these same ingredients to work for our health?! Is making money more important than our health? Let us now have a clear picture of the Christ of Health within our body-temple, and bring it into manifestation through positive confession.

Once we have a clear picture in place as to all we are and have in Christ then we are ready to *confess our* faith…giving us *victory* in *every area* of our confession. When this inner picture is so vividly established in the Word we will see these 'inner fountains' of living waters begin to usher forth beautiful words…creative words…victorious words. These will be words that cannot be *defeated!* It will be well with us, nevertheless, to *organize* our *confessions*.

It is good to write things down. Meditate on the Word and give voice to your desires…make a *specific* list…write them down. Lets make ourselves a list of clear cut confessions and give voice to all our Godly desires! Let us decree VICTORY!

We must 'see' what we want and not what we have. We must confess what we desire and not the symptom or circumstance. God tells us to "calleth those things which be not as though they *were*" (Rms. 4: 17). We think we are being 'honest' about a circumstance or a symptom we feel in our body. But, we must, nevertheless, watch what we *confess* in these instances. God tells us to 'call forth' the things we desire...even though they have not as yet manifested. If we, instead, confess the circumstance or symptom we will keep ourselves in bondage and the same rut as the world...with no vision, no faith, no words of escape. Yes, we must 'call forth' the desires of our heart from the unseen realm of God's vast storehouse of treasures. These are *all ours in Christ*. Why should we settle for anything less? Why should we settle for the same rotten fruits the world is reaping?

We are the REDEEMED! We should only be reaping God's best! *Determine* to settle for nothing less than God's best! We are certainly not giving God the glory by handing Him the same rotten fruits gathered by unbelievers. Why settle for a life of sickness and defeat when our victory is *already established* in God's NEW COVENANT sealed by the blood of Jesus? Victory is *ours to* claim…with the *positive confession* of God's victorious Word!

Let us now proceed to make a list and write out the desires of our heart. We do not need to settle for anything but God's best! Let us determine to decree God's living words over our lives! Here is a possible list of decrees:

"By faith, I decree DIVINE HEALTH for my body, in Jesus' name"

"By faith, I decree that by Jesus' stripes my _____ (name diseased organ) was healed at Calvary"

"By faith, I decree that every cell of my body is radiating the Light of Christ in perfect health"

"By faith, I decree that my body is under the blood and divinely protected from all plagues and germs, in Jesus' name"

"By faith, I decree that my body is God's property…the temple of the Holy Spirit…sanctified with the blood of Jesus"

"By faith, I decree that God's angels ever watch over me…ever protecting me, in Jesus' name"

"By faith, I decree that no plague can come nigh my dwelling...any germ that even comes close to my body dies instantly, in Jesus' name"

"By faith, I decree wisdom and creative ideas, in Jesus' name"

"By faith, I decree supernatural increase, prosperity, and the abundant life in Christ Jesus"

"By faith, I decree I have the Mind of Christ and perfect memory"

"By faith, I decree that I am debt free, in Jesus' name"

"By faith, I decree love, joy, and tranquility for my home and marriage,

"By faith, I decree salvation and deliverance for all my family and loved ones, in Jesus' name"

As we discipline our positive confession we can even call those things which 'be not' as though they 'were'. Let us get in the habit of *only positive* confession! Let us get in the habit of boldly decreeing our confessions *every* morning to begin each day...in stride and on the right foot. Let us again confess these desires every night before retiring. Each of us has our own personal needs and desires. We each have specific bills to pay, family needs of salvation and deliverance, specific areas of healing, personal circumstances to overcome, personal talents to develop and business ventures to succeed. Be specific! Make your own list. Confess! Decree God's living words over your life. The Word of God is, truly, "Quick, and powerful; and sharper than any two-edged sword" …it can even pierce into our soul and spirit, and can even do surgery on the cells of our body! "Receive with meekness the *engrafted Word—*" The Word, as only 'head knowledge', will never be engrafted into our body or into the deep regions of the soul. Be diligent. Be faithful. "Hold fast the faithful Word!" (Titus 1:9).

God says that He will give us the Keys to the Kingdom of Heaven. He says we can have these keys if we learn the principles of BINDING and LOOSING… "and whatsoever thou shalt *bind* on earth shall be bound in heaven: and whatsoever thou shalt *loose* on earth shall be loosed in heaven."

The discipline of the Art of Confession has two sides. We have discussed the positive confession of "loosing". Now we must address the question of "binding". Jesus said that, in our battle of spiritual warfare, we must bind the strong man. We bind Satan in the all-powerful *name of Jesus*. It is our responsibility, through the words of our mouth, to break the *powers of darkness!* We have been given *all authority* in *Jesus' name!* Let us now make a list of the negatives in our lives that need to be broken. Let us boldly decree:

"Satan, I bind you, and in the name of Jesus I break the powers of darkness over my mind"

"Satan, I bind you, and in the name of Jesus I break the power of the spirits of infirmity over my body"

"Satan, I bind you, and in the name of Jesus I break the power of the spirits of poverty over my finances"

"Satan, I bind you, and in the name of Jesus I break the power of all familiar spirits holding my family in the curse of bondage'

"Satan, I bind you and I break the power of sickness and all spirits of death over my family, in Jesus' name"

Again, make your own specific list of all you don't want in your life. Bind the devil and all the powers of darkness and decree freedom and *victory* in Jesus' name!

Beside our conscious confessions we must always be alert and on guard during the heat of the day as we meet life's frustrations and disappointments head on. How easy it is to let slip negative and destructive words when we feel slighted or misused. This must also become a discipline. It might even seem impossible to utter a positive confession in such instances. Don't say anything! Hold your peace! Pray 'in the Spirit'. Let *praying in tongues replace* any careless speech. When we 'pray in tongues,' we are praying in *God's language*...we are praying in God's *perfect will*. This is where we want to be! By praying in tongues we turn a negative, and a possible explosive situation, into a *positive!* If we confront an immovable mountain *pray in the Spirit* until you *pray through* to victory!

Positive confession, if *consciously* organized and disciplined, can and should become a habit. Yes, lets let victorious and successful living become a glorious habit!! It is all ours...in Christ...through the discipline of positive confession!

VII

SPIRITS OF INFIRMITY

"Healing all that were oppressed of the devil"

Acts 10: 38

God is the author of Life. Satan is the author of death. Satan has lined the path to the doorway of death with every disease and sickness imaginable. Man has placed the blame on an Invisible unknown that silently floats through windows and fills the atmosphere...the mysterious germ. But God calls it like it is...spirits of infirmity. Satan is the god of this world, and has contaminated the atmospheres with his evil spirits...and is rapidly destroying the human race. Perhaps it is time we take another look at the CAUSE of disease and stamp it with a true label: EVIL! God is the God of Life...the Way...and the Truth. His Life is the "Life more abundant". His Life is eternal. His Life is holy. His Life is love. His life is pure...undefiled by the spirits of evil. Satan breeds all his unclean spirits in the cesspools of darkness, and releases them like a swarm of killer bees on the human race.

Satan is well organized with legions of satanic spirits to do his bidding. Truly, we do not fight against flesh and blood!

Medical laboratories are researching, advertising, testing, and promoting every kind of medicine imaginable.

They continue to look only at symptoms…totally overlooking the whole man. They are attempting to cure, invisible 'germs' in the physical arena…ignoring the *spiritual realm* altogether!

All life is of SPIRITUAL origin, whether we know it or not. Medicines may alleviate some symptoms, but they are playing the game on the wrong playing field…and the spirits of infirmity are still hanging around. They are very coy. They may seem to hide or play dead…but will, sooner or later, raise their ugly heads ringing the death knoll. Yes, Satan has a well organized army. Our warfare is not carnal. The battleground is in the heavenlies. "We wrestle not against flesh and blood, but against principalities, against powers, against the rulers of the darkness of this world, against spiritual wickedness in high places" (Eph. 6: 12). We will never win the war of divine health with our head in the sand…never recognizing the real enemy…never engaging in *spiritual* warfare. We have made materialism *god*, and the medical profession lord of out body. We accept their prognosis as gospel…and completely overlook the *real* "good news" of God's Word. We often take the doctor's advice without even first checking God's word on the subject! We have disassociated ourselves from the Word of Life...continuing to live in the bondage of materialism.

Satan is having a good laugh! As long as he has us on the wrong playing field he will always 'win! We are playing according to his rules. We look at the physical body and see only physical symptoms. There is a *spiritual universe* the carnal mind does not see. There is warfare raging in the heavenlies! God open our spiritual eyes that we might see these messengers of death for what they really are! Satan will attack every part of our body. A body, unprotected by the blood of Jesus, can have any and every organ lying open to the onslaught of these demonic, infirm spirits.

Every Christian must see their body as *God's property*...God's HOLY TEMPLE! Every Christian should see every fiber and organ of their body as God's ultimate workmanship structured and forged in the creative furnaces of His "image and likeness". Every Christian must keep their eye always focused on the all-inclusiveness of God...that their entire body-temple be "full of Light" (Math. 6: 22). Every Christian must keep their body-temple covered and sanctified with the blood of Jesus. Every Christian must keep themselves saturated in the Word...making God's eternal Word the very *structure* of their life! Every Christian must *consciously* make Jesus the

LORD and *reality* of their life: spirit, soul, mind, and *body!* Yes, we must put on the full armour of God: clothed in the TRUTH of God's Word…wearing the breastplate of RIGHTEOUSNESS…walking in the glory of God's PEACE…always holding the Shield of FAITH before us…wearing the helmet of our SALVATION…and fighting the spirits of darkness with the Sword of the SPIRIT: the WORD OF GOD!

God will prove us. We *will* be tested! As a Christian, in the army of God, we will fight many spiritual battles. But, thanks be to God, we have the *victory* in Christ Jesus! The battle has *already* been won! The price of victory was paid at Calvary. The blood of Jesus has paid it all! By Jesus' stripes we *are* HEALED"! (Isaiah 53: 5). As long as we *wear* the armour, the spirits of infirmity can only fly around us in total frustration! Satan tested Jesus in the wilderness to see if He was wearing His armour. If he tested Jesus, he will surely test us! Jesus defeated him with the Sword of the Spirit: "IT IS WRITTEN". So must we!

When we are attacked in our body we seem to always run to the phone calling the doctor for help…when we should look Satan straight in the eye and say: "It is written"! We must draw the sword of the Word and go on the offensive! It is *our* responsibility to protect God's Property! Demons flee at the *name of JESUS*! Most believers have their armour in storage…and their sword rusting for lack of use. Their eyes are off God. They are worried. They see only what Satan wants them to see and feel: physical symptoms. They nervously wait for the results of lab tests and the physician's prognosis. Like babes they cry to God: "Why me"? And God wonders, in amazement, how any believer could be so stupid standing in the middle of a raging battle without his armour! God open our spiritual eyes!

Life is of the Spirit. God's armour is a spiritual armour—to protect the whole man: spirit, soul, mind, and body. Yes, our spiritual body is the WHOLE man. If we do not have our *entire* spiritual body covered and protected with God's armour our *physical* body will be completely exposed. Satan's army of unclean spirits will sworm on us like vultures looking for their next meal, and, if we let them (not carrying our shield of faith) they will pick our bones clean! We are in SPIRITUAL WARFARE (whether we know it or not) and, if we are playing the game of life on the wrong playing field, we will be subject to Satan's rules of the game! The unsaved are playing Satan's games in ignorance, but the child of God, saved by the blood, has no excuse. The born-again believer must *awaken* to the fact that God's weapons of warfare are not carnal, but mighty, to the pulling down of Satan's strongholds! We must weild the Sword of the Spirit and claim our victory, in Jesus' name! Yes, the battle has already been won on the cross of Calvary! The blood of Jesus has done it all. Nothing but the blood!

We release the power of the blood by speaking directly to Satan: "It is written". We, as Christians, are wasting our time playing the 'flesh' games of the world. It is the *speaking of the* Word that *releases* our *faith*. Jesus told those He healed that it was their *own faith* that had made them *whole*! When we release our faith, by speaking the Word, God will open *fountains of living water* from the depths of our being. The resurrection power of the Holy Spirit will be activated from the center of every cell…filling our entire body with Light. The spirits of infirmity only thrive in the stagnant pools of darkness like a sworm of mosquitoes. Ignorance *is* darkness. The spirits of infirmity will flee as we release the resurrection power of the Holy Spirit quickening every cell with the Light of Christ! The darkness of disease cannot exist in the Light.

In the ignorance of the carnal mind we only behold the physical nature of life and are mesmerized by symptoms. We do not even consider the soul, or mind, or spirit. Satan has us totally hooked on the physical symptom and has implanted it in our mind with a medical name. The symptom has blinded us to God, His spiritual universe, His Word, and the divine health we have been promised. We have allowed Satan to isolate the symptom from the whole man…delegating it to the 'physical' body only. Divine health can only be realized if *every* part of the whole man is back *in order* and in *total unity*.

Satan can only attack our body through our mind and soul. Only the will of the soul, and the conviction of the mind can put on God's armour. Without the armour the body is defenseless! When the mind is tossed and tormented in sin, the soul will become black with darkness, and the body will begin to breakdown in a steady progression of disease. The spirits of infirmity have begun to do their work. They have been given total license to destroy our body…and we, alone, are to blame. "God sent his word to heal them" (Psm-107: 20). And we left it, gathering dust, on the shelf. We didn't so much as even raise the Sword of the Spirit. The mind is the housekeeper of the body, and should have consciously worn the full armour that God gave it to wear. We have only *ourselves to blame! God's Word speaks loud and clear.*

We must take a good look at the *spiritual* nature of our lives. We must see our body in a spiritual light. We must understand the interrelationship of the spirit to the soul, to the mind, and to the body. Life is health and wholeness in the ONENESS *of God*. The soul, the mind, and the body must be totally integrated in the ONENESS OF THE SPIRIT! The Spirit of God must have *total dominion* over our lives! The break-down of the body is the result of the fracture of the whole man into countless pieces. Divine health is only found in WHOLENESS! Wholeness can only be found in the UNITY of the *Spirit*. The Spirit can only be in total control in the purity of HOLINESS. Holiness can only be purchased by the BLOOD OF JESUS. Nothing but the blood!

We have been inclined to separate 'deliverance' from 'healing'…delegating deliverance to the *mind* and healing to the *body*. The carnal mind has separated these two because it has been influenced by the symptom of the effect, and failure to see the spiritual cause. Healing is really the restoration of the body after the body has been *freed* through its deliverance from the satanic bondage of unclean spirits. Divine health is restored once deliverance is affected…whether on the spiritual, mental, or physical plane.

When the spirit of infirmity attacks our *spirit* we can see the *effect* of a rebellious spirit, the hardening of the heart to the gospel, and a dark, sinister spirit. All the powers and demons of darkness are released in the evils of murder, lusts, and hates of every description. When the spirits of infirmity attach

Christ: Our Health

themselves to our mind we can see the effect of depression, disorientation, insanity, a reprobate mind...a mind held captive. When the spirits of infirmity lodge in the *soul* we see the effect of emotional disorders, a weakening of the will, and multiple personality disorders...a soul dark and in bondage. When the spirits of infirmity attack our *body* and attach themselves to an organ, or some other area of the body, they disrupt the normal function of the intricate and complex systems of the body causing multiple possibilities of malfunction...a body breaking down in disease, unnatural stress, and pain.

The armour of God and the weapons of our warfare are both defensive and offensive. Once the window of opportunity has been opened, and the spirits have come in (whether in soul, mind, or body) we must take the weapons of our warfare, the sword of the spirit, and *deliver ourselves* by dislodging and extracting them from our person. We must take the *offensive!* We must take hold of the sword of the spirit. We must use the *authority of Jesus' name*. Once we are freed by these weapons of deliverance, we must make sure this window is *closed*...lest seven more spirits of evil come back expecting to find entrance. Once the window is closed in our defense, then the *healing process of restoration* can begin, and the Light of God's most holy Presence can once again establish His "image and likeness" …divine health!

Let us look at the deliverance of the mind (which can also have an effect on the body) as found in the eighth chapter of Luke:

"There met him out of the city a certain man, which had devils a long time, and ware no clothes, neither abode in any, house, but in the tombs. When he saw Jesus, he cried out, and fell down before him, and with a loud voice said, What have I to do with thee; Jesus, thou Son of God most high? I beseech thee, torment me not. (For he had *commanded* the *unclean spirit* to *come out* of the man. For oftentimes it had caught him: and he was kept bound with chains and in fetters; and he brake the bands, and was driven *of the* devil into the wilderness.) And Jesus asked him, saying, What is thy name? And he said, Legion: because many devils were entered into him. And they besaught him that he would not command them to go out into the deep. And there was there an herd of many swine feeding on the mountain: and they besought him that he would suffer them to enter into them. And he suffered them. Then went the devils out *of the man*, and entered into the swine: and the herd ran violently down a steep place into the lake, and were choked.

Then they went out to see what was done; and came to Jesus, and found the man, out of whom the *devils were departed*, sitting at the feet of Jesus, clothed and in *his right* mind."

Notice that Jesus, using the gift of the discernment of spirits, saw directly into the spirit realm and spoke directly to the demon within the man. And it was the demon within the man that spoke back to Jesus! Jesus identified the demon by asking its name. The demon said his name was Legion because they were many. Jesus, using His spiritual authority, commanded these unclean spirits to come out of the man. Once delivered, he was back in his right mind. He had been bound by spirits…no need of psychotherapy or group therapy!

Let us now look at the deliverance of the *body* as found in the eleventh chapter of Luke:

"And, behold, there was a woman which had a *spirit of infirmity* eighteen years, and was bowed together, and could in no wise lift up herself. And when Jesus saw her, he called her to him, and said unto her, Woman, thou art *loosed from thine infirmity.* And he laid his hands on her; and immediately she was made straight; and glorified God—"

It seems that these unclean spirits specialize in affecting certain organs or body parts. We see them often hindering hearing and speech. Jesus often commanded deaf and dumb spirits to "come out". They simply cling there, keeping that part of the body from functioning normally.

Spirits of infirmity can attack the body as well as the mind. The symptoms seem so different that most people do not realize that this devilish source is still the same!

The power of these spirits must be broken and *cast out* before *healing* (mental or physical) can begin…in the process of restoration. Satan is the author of sin, sickness, and death…and controls the spirits of infirmity that plague this planet. As long as the natural man identifies this plague of sickness to 'natural' causes and labels them with medical names, Satan will get off scott free. If we do not look at the curse of sickness, and these demonic powers, we will never be free. We will remain in bondage to the flesh and its multiple symptoms. In the fifth chapter of Acts it is recorded:

"There came a multitude out of the city bringing sick folks, and them which were vexed with unclean *spirits*: and they were healed every one—"

Satan's hold, through these unclean spirits, must be *broken in the power of Jesus'* name, and cast out through the *word of command!*

Divine health can only be realized as a lasting reality through a continuing, *ongoing* faith…a *life-style* of *spiritual living* and *walking with God.* Jesus warned those he healed that if they should continue to sin and lead a carnal life-style that more unclean spirits would return and defile their bodily housing with still more sickness. It is recorded in the eleventh chapter of Luke:

"When the unclean spirit Is gone out of a man, he walketh through dry places, seeking rest; and finding none, he saith, I will return unto my house whence I came out. And when he cometh, he findeth it swept and garnished. Then goeth be, and taketh to him seven other spirits more wicked than himself; and they enter in, and dwell there: and the last state of that man is worse than the first—"

Unclean spirits will return to a house that is empty! These spirit-germs will continue their work of destruction. We must *abide in the Word, fellowship with the Holy Spirit*, and *walk with* God if we wish to *keep* our lives *holy*, filled With *God's Presence*, and protected from Satan's destroying spirits.

It is the Word that releases the resurrection power of the Holy Spirit within the atomic structure of the cell…filling our bodily temple with Light. Satan and his powers of darkness cannot abide the Light of God's Presence! "Then shall thy Light break forth as the morning, and thine HEALTH shall spring forth speedily: and thy righteousness shall go before thee; and the glory of the Lord shall be thy reward" (Isaiah 58: 8).

The mind is the housekeeper of the body and must abide continually in the Word if the body is to remain clean and undefiled. We live in a contaminated world. "Now ye are CLEAN through the Word" (John 15: 3). Each cell is structured by God's inherent intelligence…His Omniscience. God's omniscience readily responds to God's holy Word spoken from our lips. In God's Spiritual World (His Kingdom) all things are flowing in divine harmony. When the Word of God is spoken forth in full authority it releases God's Omniscience in the cell-life…igniting the spiritual power of God's omnipotence. The divine pattern (God's "Image and likeness") in every cell and organ has never changed…and is caused to 'spring back' into its *original pattern* when *responding* to God's eternal Word! The Laws of the universe are contained in God's Word. Spiritual laws are real! We are held in bondage by our own ignorance of these Laws and their spiritual application to our lives.

Let us begin to speak forth God's eternal Word over our lives! Let us take the authority of Jesus' name and speak to our mountains…*commanding* them to move! Let us speak God's healing words right into the very heart of cell-consciousness…bringing it back into its original structure of perfection! Let us speak the Word and bind Satan, and command the powers of darkness to be broken…forbidding any malfunction of any organ! Let us speak directly to these spirits of infirmity and command them "OUT" in Jesus' name! God's holy temple should not be defiled! It is God's workmanship…made in His own image and likeness!

Let us *continually* affirm the Word:

"MY body is the temple of the living God"

"I apply the blood of Jesus Christ to my spirit, my soul, my mind, and my body"

"My whole man is totally sanctified by the blood of Jesus"!

"Every organ of my body is made in the perfection of God's image and likeness, and every organ is now functioning in that perfection"

"Every cell of my body radiates the Light of Christ…my body is filled with radiant Light"

"Christ hath REDEEMED me from the curse of sickness"

"Jesus took my infirmities and bore my sickness"

"By Jesus' stripes I *am* healed"

"I forbid any infirm spirit to infect my body-temple…for my body is God's property"

"The Blood of Jesus covers my body and mind protecting and insulating them from every demon of sickness and every evil force"

"Every atom and cell of my body vibrates in God's original pattern of perfection and divine harmony"

"The Life of Jesus is manifest in every cell and organ of my body"

"Every cell of my body is composed of God's Omnipresence, God's Omniscience, and God's Omnipotence"

"God's Word abides in me...totally saturating the cell—consciousness of every organ and fiber of my body"

"I forbid any malfunction of any organ of my body"

"The blood of Jesus washes and sanctifies every cell in the purity of holiness"

"I command the powers of darkness be broken and every unclean spirit "OUT" in Jesus' name"!

"Every atom of my body-temple vibrates God's eternal love"

"Every cell of my body is sanctified unto the Lord…washed in the blood of the Lamb"

"My body is made in God's image and likeness, and I claim Divine Health, in Jesus' name"

"The Spirit of Life in Christ Jesus hath made me free from the curse of sin, sickness and death"

"The resurrection power of the Holy Spirit is being released and is now quickening every cell in Divine Health"

"My whole man: spirit, soul, mind, and body is holy unto the Lord…in the perfect order and alignment of divine harmony and total health"!

Amen

VIII

TAKING AUTHORITY

"And gave them *power* and *authority* over all devils, and to cure diseases"

Luke 9: 1

Jesus said, "Ye shall receive power, after the Holy Ghost is come upon you—" Those believers who have received this great and marvelous power have been given God's authority to use it in proclaiming the gospel of Jesus Christ. This is the mandate of every born-again, spirit-filled Christian. The world would have been saved long ago if the church had truly assumed its high position of authority and power. Instead, the church chose to avoid the great confrontation with the powers of darkness and chose, instead, to become a pious, religious organization of doctrine, creeds, and ceremonies. Somewhere, many centuries ago, the church came to a fork in the road and parted company with the Holy Spirit, and God's plan for His church. On the day of Pentecost, God poured His Spirit out upon the expectant believers that they might have the power and authority to take back by force all that the devil had stolen from the human race… "and gave them power and authority over all devils, and to cure diseases." (Luke 9: 1). The church, however, became so carnal minded that it never really understood the spiritual warfare raging in the spiritual domain devastating the lives of humanity in every conceivable way. Paul wrote to the believers at Corinth: "That your faith should not stand in the wisdom of men, but in the power of God." (I Cor. 2:5). Yes, our faith should be in the "demonstration of the Spirit and power."

Where has the power gone? By not exercising its authority the church has let this power seep out between the cracks of its closed doors…searching for expression in the lives of believers ready and willing to do battle. The battle is raging full force in these last days. When will the church wake up?! When will we take up the sword of authority and enter the battle and fulfill these final words of Jesus to His church: "In my name shall they cast out devils; they shall speak with new tongues; they shall take up serpents; and if they drink any deadly thing, it shall not hurt them; they shall lay hands on the sick, and they shall recover." (Mark 16: 17, 18). This Commission of Jesus to His followers was a command! This was not a suggestion to be ignored. The church has turned a deaf ear to this Great Commission…and is still nursing its sick and burying its dead. It has willfully chosen to ignore the battle, and walk the way of least resistance…justifying itself by preaching morality and good works. While its head is in the sand, Satan and his powers of darkness are ravaging and destroying this world beyond recognition…and, if the church doesn't wake up, he will take the church down with it! The church can never be triumphant if it doesn't enter the battle, take its position of authority, put on the full armour of God, and defeat the enemy of God.

Our authority is in the Word, but we must take it at face value…live it…and act upon it. If the Word tells us to "cast out devils" then we must recognize the fact that there are devils, and *do* something about them. It is for *us* to take action…through the directive and power of the Holy Spirit. God has given us His authority in Jesus' name and tells *us* to use it. Jesus said that the 'works' that He has done *we* can do also…even greater works! Why aren't we doing the greater works? If our body is sick and racked with pain why do we continue to succumb to these demonic attacks when the scripture plainly tells us that Christ hath REDEEMED us from the curse of sickness, and that by "Jesus' stripes we are healed"? Have we sunk so low that we do not even recognize that sickness is a part of the curse and is from the devil?

It is time we begin to truly know the WORD for *ourselves* and *take authority*. God and His Word are one. Jesus is the 'Word made flesh'. The worlds were framed by the Word of

God! It is our defense. It is our *weapon of battle*. It is our *authority*. It is our *victory!* The Word can only take effect in our lives and be a creative power by our *knowing* it,..*speaking* it, *doing* it, and *living* it. This is the only way we can win the battle!

We all have tests and trials…mountains to overcome. Jesus said that we must literally *speak to our mountains*, take the position of authority, and command them to move out of our lives! This could be a financial mountain, a cancerous mountain, or anything Satan has set up as a roadblock to keep us from the victorious life Jesus paid to give us. He paid the ultimate price with His own blood to give us, as a free gift of grace, the abundant life He promised. We must take our position of authority if we are to receive from God. Jesus told us to have total *faith in God*: "For verily I say unto you, that whosoever shall *say* unto this *mountain, Be thou removed*, and be thou cast into the sea; and shall *not doubt in his heart, but shall believe* that those things which he saith shall come to pass; he shall have *whatsoever he saith*. Therefore I say unto you, What things soever ye desire, when ye pray, *believe* that ye *receive* them, and ye shall have them", (Mark 11: 23, 24).

Jesus tells us to do something about our illness. He tells *us* to take *authority*. He tells *us* to command our mountains! We have lost our faith in God and His promises of health. We have placed our lives (and our faith) in the hands of the medical. We have closed our eyes to Satan, the destroyer, and his demons of destruction. We have not entered the battle. We have not taken our position of authority in Christ (only a horizontal, bed-ridden position). God wants His people strong and healthy…ready to march against the enemy. How we have failed and grieved the heart of God!

How do we go about taking the position of authority for our health? Here are the ten steps of authority:

1. Have faith *in God*. Read, study, and know the Word. God and His Word are ONE. Search out all the scriptural promises of health and healing.
2. Recognize that all sickness and disease is from Satan. He goes about seeking those he can destroy. His demons of disease are always attacking. *He is the enemy.*
3. Claim God's *Covenant of health* and promises of healing: "Christ hath redeemed me from the curse of sickness." "By Jesus' stripes I *am* healed."

4. *Bind Satan. Command* the powers of darkness be *broken* off your life. Command the spirits of infirmity to "go" from your body!

5. *Speak* to your *mountain* (whatever the sickness may be). If it is a cancer curse it at its roots and command it to die. Command the cancer (mountain) to dry up and cast it from your body, in Jesus' name! (Remember, speak *directly* to the cancer or whatever the illness may be).

6. Thank God for the Blood of Jesus ever flowing through your body washing away all sin, all germs, all disease…*sanctifying* every cell in the *purity of holiness*.

7. Praise God that your body is the *Temple* of the Holy Spirit and must not be defiled. Protect it with the 'Blood covering' at all cost.

8. Thank God that your body is filled with the power of the Holy Spirit *quickening* every cell in *divine health*. "If the Spirit of Him that raised Jesus from the dead *dwell in you*, he that raised up Christ from the dead shall also *quicken your* mortal *bodies by his Spirit* that *dwelleth in you*" (Rms 8: 11).

9. *Praise* God for *divine health in Christ* Jesus! Jesus lives in me. He is my all in all.

10. Thank God that the *Life of Jesus* is made manifest in your mortal flesh (II Cor. 4:10, 11). "I live; yet not I, but *Christ liveth in* me" (Gal. 2: 20). "Christ is *magnified in my body*" (Phil. 1:20). My body-temple is filled with the *Light of Christ. My body radiates the Glory of God!*

Yes, we must take authority over our mountains. Command them to move. Satan has infected our body-temple with his 'mountains' of disease. These mountains have no legal right in God's body-temple. Speak to your mountains! Jesus always spoke commands when it came to sickness. He took authority over the devil. He commanded every mountain of disease to be removed. He has given His authority to His body, the church, upon the earth.

God has given *you* this authority! Take it. It's yours!

IX

THE CHANNEL: BODY AND SOUL

It is time we, as Christians, take a good look at our body and at our soul. Generally speaking, we have looked at the body as a very complex, physical, biological organism…something we cannot begin to comprehend. We have totally identified our life with the body…pinning to it all the identification tags of looks, family, intelligence, social status, friends, occupation, talents, etc.. In the back of our mind we sense that life is fleeting and temporal…and watch the body slowly marching to its destiny—the open grave. We look out, from the eyes of the body, and see an ever changing, relative world…and have bent and shaped our life to fit into the mold of society and this 'outer' world. Through our limited vision we see only surface imagery…and have become mesmerized to the physical world of appearances…which includes the body.

We sense there must be a soul…but don't really know what it is. The soul is something we just don't seem to understand…a very nebulous 'inner something' at best. We know we have it, but can't really define it. We can better understand the soul by breaking it down into its component parts. The soul is a three part entity: mind, emotion, and will. We are intelligent/feeling beings directed by free-will. The soul is the middle ground of man's triune makeup: spirit, soul, and body. The soul is the battleground. Satan is vying for the soul of man. Satan will do anything in his power to influence the mind and the free-will of man. Because the soul is stationed between the spirit and the body it can face the will, in its free state, either toward the spirit or toward the body. By keeping the will facing the body and, consequently, the 'world' (as manifesting through the senses) it subjects the soul to all that is carnal. Because Satan is the god of this world, he is holding man spellbound to the world with all its sensual and sinful living. It seems that there is a great percentage of believers who God has labeled "carnal Christians". This, nevertheless, is a label we all can grow out of as we strike out on the path of spiritual growth, and turn our will to face our spirit. We will only come to know Jesus, the author of our life, by facing His Spirit within us. Our spirit embraces the Holy Spirit…and it is through the Holy Spirit that we have direct access into God's Kingdom.

In seeking health and healing for our body, we seem to have totally divorced it from the soul. This is because we categorize the body as 'physical' and the soul as more 'spiritual'. This is also because the medical profession only treats the body and its symptoms. By treating only the symptom is has failed to find the

Source. By treating only the body it has failed to realize the significant relationship between body and the soul. "Beloved, I wish above all things that thou prosper and be in health, even as thy *soul* prospereth". Here we see that John is showing us the direct connection and interrelationship of soul to the body…the health of the body being directly related to the well-being of the soul. Could it be that the body is somehow connected to the soul? Could it be that the body is the 'physical' extension and expression of the soul? Could it be we will never find the source of the body's physical ailments if we never look to see where the soul is hurting?

Could it be that the body is merely expressing the in-harmony and dis-ease of the soul? Perhaps its time we look to the soul…and fix it! Perhaps its time we focus first on the healing of the soul…and watch the physical symptoms disappear! Could it be that a distraught soul is expressing the bodily symptom of nervous stress? Could it be that a soul torn by unforgiveness gives rise to all kinds of heart problems? Could it be that a soul filled with hate gives rise to spiteful growths and cancers? This disconnect of soul and body can produce an endless list. The medical profession continues to document countless symptoms…and the source, the soul, is completely overlooked. God is concerned for the soul of man. It could well be that to get the body *really* healed the soul must first be healed. God wants the soul healed!

The principal cause of the separation of soul and body is the conception that the body is but a physical, biological entity composed of cell formations. It is time we take another look at the body…and see it in a more *spiritual* light. The truth of the matter is that the 'physical' world, as we know it, as assembled and assimilated in consciousness, is in appearance only. The physical, as we know it, is but surface imagery. If we could possess spiritual, x-ray vision we could see right through the cell, to the molecule, to the atom, to the electron, to magnetic fields of Light, to Spiritual Reality itself! At this point, we would only recognize the body as *spirit* (as seen through a giant x-ray machine). This spirit-body is composed of God's Omnipresence, God's Omniscience, and God's Omnipotence! God is all in all…in and through all things. God is Spirit. God projected everything onto the plane of physical expression from His own Spirit! When we can open our eyes and see the *spiritual reality* of all life then we can see the true relationship of soul and body…the body being the 'physical' vehicle and extension of the soul! When we can see through the solid appearance of matter and behold only God's Presence we will begin to appreciate our body as God's workmanship…His holy temple.

When we realize the cell-life as composed of God's omnipresence, omniscience and omnipotence we can more easily see how the Word works in the restoration of the body. God's omniscience in each cell will readily respond to God's own Word! The Word, like a giant spiritual magnet, will realign the diseased cells of inharmony into straight lines. God's Word expresses His Life…His Love. When we appropriate, and consciously inject God's Word and Love into the cell life the cells will respond…singing God's praises of health. Jesus said that even the rocks would sing out. Yes, God's body-temple is composed of 'lively stones,'…a spiritual house.

It has been said that the mind is the housekeeper of the body. The cells of the body will never truly vibrate in the manifesting health of pure spirit if the mind remains carnal. We must become 'spiritually minded' if we ever expect to see the spiritualization of the body. The cells of the body must vibrate in the harmony of pure spirit…if we ever wish to live in the dimension of divine health. Jesus told those he healed that it was their faith that made them *whole*. Jesus, the Word of Life, raised the level of their faith so that the body, in turn, could respond to the Word by instantly realigning the atoms into their original order of spiritual wholeness. Their faith responded to the *Word*, and their *body* responded to their faith! Our health and wholeness is *established in our* faith. Without faith, the cell-life will continue to break down and deteriorate in a state of spiritual inharmony…dis-ease. "God sent His Word and healed them!" God's Word releases His Spirit to restore wholeness. All things must line up to the Word. Jesus spoke the Word and even the elements of nature responded…the storm ceased and the waves became calm. God created the universe with His Word: "Let there be". God's resounding Words of Life continue to echo through the corridors of time…ever controlling, ever regulating, ever creating. God's Word still holds the universe together in exacting precision. God's Words are a powerful two-edged sword. When Jesus returns to planet earth He will simply destroy His enemies by the Word of His mouth…streaming forth Light as a giant, spiritual sword! Let us begin to use His Words of Life and begin to work some spiritual surgery on ourselves! Like a giant laser beam God's Word will cut away and restore the body to its original conception of wholeness.

God created man in His own image and likeness…and perfection. Man was never made to be sick. Sickness came by the curse of sin. Adam, and his lineage, was severed from the presence of God's loving Spirit with God's curse ringing in his ears. From that day on man's soul was lost, his mind was in torment, and his body labored. His body grew sick with the curse of sin. By sin came death. He was living a slow death! The cells became void of God's everlasting Light…degenerating into the shadows…a gradual state of decomposition. Spiritually speaking, Jesus never left His glorified body. Even when He walked this earth He never lived in the cursed dimension of death. He and His Father were one: spirit, soul, mind, and body. Jesus' mind and body were totally incorporated into the oneness of the Father…in spiritual wholeness. There is no separation in wholeness. Our health *is* our *wholeness!* Jesus' soul and body were completely united in wholeness…spiritual unity. Yes, we must begin to take another look at the relation of soul and body. Let us raise our vision and grasp this revelation of *oneness!* Without a vision people perish.

The oneness of soul and body is bound in the oneness of spiritual unity. It all begins with the direction of the *will*. Every minute of the day our free-will is confronted with choices…choices that choose the paths we walk…choices that could determine our eternal destiny. To be carnally minded is death, but to be *spiritually minded* is life and peace. As unbelievers, our will was in a continual state of hypnosis…totally mesmerized to the outside world of appearances…always drawing from the material world it lived through the senses. Our life was based on sense perception and sense reception…the carnal life of sensuality. The believer must constructively use his free-will to turn from the lusts of the flesh and commit to the discipline of looking inward to his newly born *spirit*. It is only through his spirit does he have direct access to the Holy Spirit and the open door leading to the vast dimensions of God's Kingdom. Jesus said: "The Kingdom of God is *within* you". We will never lock into the spiritual things of God by looking out to the world. God's Kingdom of the Spirit is only found within…in the dimension of our own consciousness! We must forsake the pleasures of the world and focus our will on the things of God. The Christian walk is a walk of commitment. We must commit to the work and discipline of *keeping* our free-will from wandering…keeping it *facing the Spirit*. The Spirit must always have the place of domin*ance*. Our three-part man will only realize *wholeness* if the spirit is in the position of dominance…aligning spirit, soul, and body in perfect order. God's universe of Light only shines forth unity…all parts dissolving in the oneness of Light…all fragments drawn into the orbit of God's eternal Love. God's universe is a universe of order. God's universe of atoms orbit in exacting precision. Sin could never exist in this domain of Light. All dis-ease dissolves in the divine harmony of God's all-encompassing Presence.

When the soul becomes divinely 'tuned' to God's Spirit it begins to awaken and open as a beautiful flowering petal. Only an open soul can channel the flow of God's Spirit. When Jesus was touched by the woman with the issue of blood He said that virtue (healing power) had gone out of Him. Jesus, soul was always open to the flow of the Spirit. The faith of the woman opened her soul to receive healing virtue of the Holy Spirit as it flowed forth from the open soul of Jesus. It was her faith that had made her whole. It was through her own *open soul* that the Spirit of God flowed to restore her body. Only through her soul! Her body, otherwise, would never have been healed. Like an electric circuit, when her soul opened the circuit was completed and the power flowed…and the body was restored to wholeness. Our *health* is our *wholeness*…as the circuit is completed in the perfect alignment of spirit, soul, and body. Only through the channel of an open soul (facing the Light of God's Spirit) can the spirit flow into the body. Without the soul-food of Spirit the body decomposes in a state of spiritual malnutrition. The human race is starving for spiritual nourishment. God's healing virtue will automatically flow once the circuit of spirit, soul, and body is completed.

God's universe is a universe of Law and Order…bonded in spiritual unity. God's universe is a universe of

Love…expressing His.glory. God's universe is a universe of the Omnipresence…the eternal Reality. When the soul and body are lifted up into the glorious dimension of the Spirit in divine unity then the soul will magnify the glory of the Lord…and the body will radiate health.

X

FORGIVENESS: RELEASING THE FLOW

The life of Jesus shone forth God's original dream for a loving race of people formed in His own image and likeness. He shed His own blood for our freedom from sin's bondage. Jesus was God's life shining forth God's love and holiness…the sinless life. He walked the earth…but lived in the Spirit. He was in the world, but not of it. He lived in the dimension of Spiritual Reality…in constant fellowship and communion with His Heavenly Father. He spent long hours with His Father in prayer. His disciples, sensing the super-natural power emitting from His prayer life, asked Jesus to teach them how to pray. Jesus stressed to them the importance of a one on one intimacy with God, and for them to think of Him as He did…a loving Father.

"After this manner therefore pray ye: Our Father which art in heaven, Hallowed be thy name. Thy kingdom come. Thy will be done in earth, as it is in heaven. Give us this day our daily bread. And forgive us our debts, as we forgive our debtors. And lead us not into temptation, but deliver us from evil: For thine is the Kingdom, and the power, and the glory, forever. Amen. For if ye forgive men their trespasses, your heavenly Father will also forgive you. But if ye forgive not men their trespasses, neither will your Father forgive your trespasses." (Math. 6: 9-16)

Notice the importance Jesus gives to *forgiveness*. Not only is it an important part of the Lord's Prayer, but His primary thought following the prayer. Why is forgiveness of such grave importance? God created man in His own 'image and likeness'…a divine being…harmonious, whole, and perfect. He was conceived in God's mind, plucked from His soul, and created from His Spirit. He embodied God's life of HOLINESS. But sin severed the soul of man from its very source. Sin created a wall of separation…separating man's very life and existence from his Creator. Man's soul cried out for a Savior. Life without God became a world of darkness…a living hell.

Disease was man's fallen state…the chaos of in-harmony and dissonance…an incomplete and lost being. Man is saved by the BLOOD…and healed by the BLOOD. Jesus paid for the salvation of man's soul by the nails in His hands, and purchased his health by the stripes on his back: "And with His stripes we are HEALED" (Isaiah 53-5). God does not say we can be, or might be, or will be…He says we ARE healed! We receive our salvation *by* faith in the redemptive work of the Cross, and we receive our *healing* by this *same faith*.

Christ *has already* purchased our healing! It is only for us to CLAIM IT by faith…and realize divine *health* as a *way of* life! If Christ hath "redeemed us from the curse of the law" (including sickness)-then why are so many Christians sick?! Christ has already purchased our health! It is ours in the heavenly realm waiting our hands *of faith* to CLAIM, and bring it down and into this physical body. Why is it that so many Christians, who believe in healing, still live in sickness with all the unbelievers? What is blocking the transportation of our health in the heavenlies (where it is already established) to this earthly plane where we live? All life streams forth as a spiritual river ever flowing from the Throne of God manifesting this material plane of matter. It must flow *unhindered*…in the pure river of Light and Holiness. Yes, God's Spirit is like a flowing river manifesting God's nature in all Creation. This flow of life (and health) must remain OPEN and never be clogged with the debris of sin and unforgiveness. This is why Jesus stressed forgiveness and love.

God cannot, by His very nature of holiness, hear prayers offered in the sin of unforgiveness. The hindrances of unforgiveness simply block the answer. "If I regard iniquity in my heart, the Lord will not hear me" (Psm 66: 18). A heart hardened in unforgiveness will stop the flow. Yes, all life is as a flowing river...a river of pure Love...flowing from its Source, and back to its Origin. A heart of unforgiveness stops the flow of God's Spirit, and prevents the manifestation of our healing. Healing is ours through the blood of Jesus...but we must undam life's flowing river of all the obstacles of sin and unforgiveness imbedded deep within our lives.

Life is for the *giving!* We can only flow with the flow as we *give out* God's life. Those that live for themselves, and to themselves will struggle against life's currents...living the 'getting' life of selfishness and unrepented sins. Unforgiveness will become that big, spiritual stumbling stone that will block the flow to heal, and prevent the total manifestation of health.

Most of us are so caught up in ourselves, and our own little 'worlds', that we are hardly aware of our unrepented sins and secret faults. We have neatly shut them behind closed doors. If we truly want the river of health to flow into our lives we must humble ourselves before the Throne of God and seek God to shine His searchlight into all the dark and hidden areas of our soul. We must ask Him to reveal to our conscious mind all our secret sins, faults, and areas of unforgiveness. Only when we *repent* and *consciously remove* these stumbling blocks will God hear and answer our prayers for healing. Only when we truly forgive others will we, ourselves, come back into a harmonious relationship with our loving Father. We must consciously and systematically remove every sin that would hinder the flow of God's life to and through us. Forgiveness is the door to freedom from bondage and unanswered prayers.

God has "blessed us with every SPIRITUAL blessing." it is all ours in "heavenly places" …purchased by the blood of Jesus. Our healing, however, will never *manifest* on this physical plane if we do not even know it is ours…if we do not claim it by faith…and if we do not *forgive* and remove all the obstructions that would prevent its flow into our lives as the manifest reality of health.

Let us determine NOW to *forgive* and live a life of *unconditional* love…and begin to release the flow of God's great river of life and health!

XI

OBEDIENCE

"My son, attend to my words, incline thine ear unto my sayings. Let them not depart from thine eyes; keep them in the midst of thine heart. For they are LIFE unto those that find them, and HEALTH to all their flesh"

Prov. 4: 20-22

God's Word Is His Law. Our health and well being is intertwined in the very fabric of Divine Law. God's Word is the Law of the universe…the physics of every atom. God's universal Law *requires* obedience! His Laws cannot be transgressed…for the very universe is structured in divine order and harmony. Even the laws of nature produce inharmonious and negative *effects* if violated. Science is man's way of categorizing and testing God's infallible laws of nature…clearly showing that for every CAUSE there is a corresponding EFFECT.

Man cannot hope to live a life of health if he continually breaks God's laws and is ever reaping all the side effects. God's laws of nature are built into the very core of creation itself…including our body. This Law is Intuitively known through obedience to God's Word, and our sensitive listening to His 'still small voice' within. We must become sensitized to the leadings and direction of the Holy Spirit. God even set His Laws in stone and gave His people ten basic commandments that even a child cannot miss. He has filled the holy scriptures with instruction as to the proper care and nourishment of spirit, soul, mind, and body. Nevertheless, man, in his disobedience, has chosen to live by his own rules. He has broken every law and set up his self-gratifying ego as the 'lord' of his life. He has chosen to live in the lusts and pleasures of the flesh…opening himself to every whim and attack of Satan. He has totally ignored God's built-in laws of health for his body and corrupted it with every sin imaginable. His glorious body, which God created in His own image and likeness, has degenerated into the dark shadows of a 'living death'.

God's Laws are all incorporated in His Omnipresence. Built into this Spiritual essence is His Omniscience…the supreme intelligence inherent in all Law. It is God's Omniscience that controls all power…His Omnipotence. God's eternal Laws regulate all things on both the spiritual and physical planes. We have labeled physical manifestation the 'laws of nature'. Man can never abide in the perfection of Spiritual Law and continue to break the lower laws of nature. We must be totally obedient to

God's spiritual laws if natural law is to work for the well-being of our physical body. God has birthed us all with common sense. It does not take much sense to recognize the body's inherent need for sunshine, rest, nutrition, and exercise. This is something we all 'sense' as natural to the body in its interaction to the environment. Yet, we willfully ignore even natural law...choosing not to see all the 'effects' of these broken laws upon our body on down the road. We choose only to allow our sensual appetites to rule...and live happily for the moment. We close the books on God's laws with our 'so what' attitude...and continue in a life-style of self gratification...deterioration...and ultimate destruction.

The more we become sensitive to the leadings and guidance of the Holy Spirit, enjoying the Presence of the Lord, the more we will live a life dedicated to Him and committed to His Word (Law). We will become sensitized to nature's laws in the care of our body. Only a fool would allow Satan the right to systematically destroy his own body! Nevertheless, we see man trapped in the habits of alcohol, drugs, tobacco, etc. in the destruction of both his soul and body. God *requires* OBEDIENCE—to both His *spiritual* and natural laws! These higher and lower laws control separate planes, and, yet, are totally interrelated. One cannot be obedient to one and break the other. A broken law can only bring bondage...whether it be spiritual or physical. Young people today are being taught that there are no absolutes...everything is relative...do your 'own thing'...be free! To believe this lie from the pit of hell can only lead to a life of bondage...a life-style ignorantly breaking God's spiritual and natural laws...a life time reaping all the destroying effects of broken Law. God requires obedience. The universal laws holding this universe together cannot be broken. God's spiritual and natural laws are all contained in His WORD. Man has no excuse! God commands obedience to His Word. This is an ABSOLUTE! Man is a free agent. He can live his life his own way or God's way. Even a Christian has free choice...and can choose, if he so desires, to ignore God's Laws as set forth in His Word. It is easy for a Christian to be lazy and not bother to read and know the very laws in God's Word controlling his life. Law is law regardless of our awareness of its absolute authority. Divine health is totally dependent on our obedience to these higher and lower laws. These laws must be totally incorporated into a Christian *life-style of OBEDIENCE!* No one 'gets by' with anything...even if it be the slightest infraction of God's universal Law. For *every* Cause there is an Effect! For every broken Law there is a corresponding EFFECT on the negative side of the ledger. Eternal Law is built into the fabric of this universe and cannot be compromised by our ignorance. If we wish to live a life free of bondage then we must take the time to know the Word...and commit ourselves to *keep* it! God cannot even break His own Laws! He has promised to "lead us into all truth" through His Word and the gentle leadings of the Holy Spirit.

We must seek the Holy Spirit for wisdom concerning the laws of nature. We have been led down many dead end streets by misleading and absolutely false labels and advertisements. We have become conditioned to buy into just about anything and everything. Thank God for the Holy Spirit! The Holy Spirit knows! He is our guide into "all truth". Man will lead us down dead end alleys, but the Holy Spirit leads us always toward the Light! We must discipline ourselves in the holy communion of prayer, and *much* time fellowshipping with the Holy Spirit. We will never come to know the 'still small voice' of this dear friend if we do not spend *intimate* time with Him. He will illumine our minds with the Truth. He is the Source of all revealed knowledge. His omniscience holds the universe of atoms in exacting patterns...in precisioned, preset orbits. If these eternal Laws were discarded the universe would explode! God's universal Laws are *built in*. He is not imposing His Will on us just to see us sweat. His Law *is* our freedom…when we learn *obedience!*

How much should we exercise? What should we eat? How much rest does our body require? Should we supplement with vitamins? Life is a road *of choices.* If we listen to all the advertisements and propaganda of the airwaves we will live in a state of hopeless confusion. Only the rebirthed spirit of a born-again believer is capable of only *right* choices! Yes, the Holy Spirit within will constantly lead…if we stay yielded to His guidance. We must learn to never make a decision without first consulting the Holy Spirit! He, alone, knows what is best for *us!* We must be careful to keep ourselves *always* "in the spirit". The 'flesh' will profit us nothing. All exercise, all diets, all supplements, all methods and plans will have little *lasting* value, anyway, if only done 'in the flesh'. Only the Holy Spirit, dwelling on the inside of us, truly knows what our particular life needs…spirit, soul, mind, and body. Only the Holy Spirit will keep the whole man in tact. Man's ways are not God's ways. The 'flesh' of the carnal mind will try anything to outwardly beautify the body (in two easy lessons)…and, at the same time, allow the mind to run wild, and totally ignore the well-being and salvation of the soul!

Christ: Our Health

True and lasting health is the manifestation of *wholeness*, and *holiness*. True health must be incorporated in one's total *lifestyle!* How can a person *stay* healed if his life is 'out of sink' with the laws and purposes of God? How can a person maintain health if His life is cut off from the Life of his Creator? We have been given a *new* life in Christ Jesus!! It is *our responsibility* to live this new life...to walk in the Spirit...to stay *in Christ*. "Put on the *new man*, which after God is created in righteousness and *true holiness*" (Eph. 4: 24). The darkness of *sin* and sickness cannot exist in the *light* of a life lived *in holiness*. "For ye were sometimes darkness, but now are ye Light in the Lord: walk as *children of Light*" (Eph. 5: 8). A tumor can be surgically removed or possibly healed through the power of prayer, but if the overall lifestyle remains "sometimes darkness" the shadows of disease will eventually again close in at another time and another place. Divine health must be looked at from the standpoint of the total man rather than a temporary symptom in need of healing. When the total man is made whole; one with God; filled with Light; and radiating God's love and glory then the inharmony of sin and disease will be no more. "Till we all come in the unity of faith, and of the knowledge of the Son of God, unto a PERFECT MAN, unto the measure of the stature of the *fullness of Christ*" (Eph. 4: 13).

We, alone, are responsible for making Jesus the LORD of our lives...Lord of our mind; Lord of our body; Lord of our circumstances; Lord of our choices—of all we think or *do!*

He can only live His life in and through us when we consciously *commit our lives to His lordship*. "Until Christ be formed in you" (Gal. 4: 19). This 'forming' process is the inner *work of the Holy Spirit. We must come to know Him so personally* that we will give Him *free reign* in the lordship of our lives. In obedience we must listen to His quiet voice on the inside of us ever leading. In obedience we must obey His directives...what to do, what to eat, when to rest, where to go, how to minister! We, as Christians, have failed in this most important relationship...our intimacy with the Holy Spirit. He is the *power of manifestation*...even the manifestation of our health! We must commune with Him on a *continual* basis *throughout the day*. Every moment of the day is filled with decisions and choices...and we must give them all to Him...walking the walk of faith. The more we know *the Word* the more sensitive we will be to His leadings and lordship. The Holy Spirit will never go against God's Word. He will always lead us in line with the Word...in the fulfilling of divine Law. We can only live *in Christ* through the *resurrection power of the*

Holy Spirit. Anything outside the 'in Christ' life will give rise to sin, and its free radical offspring of disease.

Divine health is not some man-made formula or miracle cure. It is a life to be lived...committed to Christ, lived in Christ,...and expressing Christ's life of absolute purity, health, and love.

XII

WASHING OF THE BLOOD

Every born-again Christian knows that he or she was 'saved' by the blood of Jesus…God's sacrificial lamb of Calvary. God's Son shed His own blood for the remission of our sins, and our eternal salvation. This was the ultimate and final sacrifice. This was the blood of the New Testament…God's glorious plan of redemption. Only blood could wash away the sins of man. God's final sacrifice was prepared in the heavens…for all eternity. "Without shedding of blood is no remission" (Heb. 9: 22). "For by one offering he hath perfected for ever them that are sanctified" (Heb. 10: 14) Jesus suffered on the cross for the remission of our sins. He carried His own blood into the heavenlies and presented it to God…as the supreme sacrifice for all mankind.

There is power in the blood. There is power in the blood to save; to heal; to cleanse; to sanctify; to empower; to protect; to defeat the enemy. We are all thankful for our salvation, but are ignorant in terms of the *application* of the blood to our everyday lives…for overcoming and victorious living…even for our health! We have failed to bring the glorious principles of the New Covenant right down here to earth in application to our

Christ: Our Health

lives. Jesus' blood bought our salvation...a salvation that *includes everything*...everything we will ever need down here to live the victorious life of divine provision, divine health, divine protection, etc. "We are COMPLETE in Him"! The blood has paid it all!...but we must see it *manifest* in our lives by *claiming* and *appropriating* it by FAITH.

We must begin to *consciously* apply the blood to *every area* of our lives...that we be sanctified in soul, mind, and body. Even though our *spirit* has been born-again in our salvation, we still find ourselves in physical bondage...contaminated by a contaminated world. It will take continuous *cleansing* by the blood of Jesus to cleanse the 'world' from our system. God requires HOLINESS! Nothing but the blood has the *power* to cleanse—not psychology, not education, not religion—nothing but the BLOOD OF JESUS! *Righteousness* will never be realized without the washing of the blood...lest we ever be bound to the lusts of the flesh. "That the righteousness of the law might be fulfilled in us, who walk not after the flesh, but *after the Spirit*. For they that are after the flesh do mind the things of the flesh, but they that are after Spirit the things of the Spirit. For to be carnally minded is death; but to be spiritually minded is life and peace" (Rms. 8: 4-6). The 'flesh' of the world will never see God. It will take the blood of Jesus to cleanse the sin-flesh that it be free to rise up in the SPIRIT...and see Him face to face! It can only be done through the *spiritual power* of the Blood! The blood of Jesus has *paid it* all...but we must APPROPRIATE it!

The blood is the POWER OF CLEANSING. The blood is empowered by the *Spirit*, activated by our Faith, and appropriated by our *Words*. Even the Christian must rise up out of the Carnal things of this world, and become 'spiritually minded'. It will take a real cleansing from the contaminations of our carnal nature to truly 'walk in the Spirit'. We will never experience overcoming and victorious living if we do not walk in God's Spirit. We will never experience divine health by continuing our carnal life-style and walking with the world. Divine health is only realized *IN Christ*...a life sanctified and made holy by the blood of Jesus. To live 'in Christ' is to walk *in the Spirit*, ever doing the Father's Will, and abiding in His love. The Christ-life can only be the Love-life. Jesus must be LORD over our souls, our minds, and our bodies. Let us learn to cleanse ourselves through the appropriation of the Lord's blood. We must truly appreciate its value and its power if we are to effectively *apply* it to our lives.

It is our 'faith that makes us *whole*,...but with most believers their faith is just sitting on the shelf. They are not *activating* their faith on a *daily* basis. They have never been taught the art *of appropriation*. Our faith must be forcefully and *consciously* applied…the 'releasing' of our faith! Again, the Blood is empowered by the Spirit, activated by our faith, and appropriated by our words. We can begin to walk in the supernatural if we begin to put these three ingredients to work in our lives. "Faith cometh by hearing, and hearing by the WORD of God" (Rms. 10: 17). In like manner, the power of faith is released by speaking the Word of God— "Whosoever shall *say* unto this mountain—" When we *speak forth* our faith we will begin to see *spiritual power* work the *laws of manifestation*. Faith must become a *tangible*…the realization of our dreams and desires. "Now *faith* is the SUBSTANCE of *things* hoped for, the evidence of things not seen" (Heb. 11: 1).

When we actually experience and see spiritual power *manifesting* in our lives then we can begin to enjoy victorious living…taking our place of authority in God's Kingdom. We will find ourselves following the world, like everyone else, if we leave our faith on the shelf gathering dust. If we are not *daily* WALKING IN THE SPIRIT, and sensitive to *every move* of the Holy Spirit, we won't have enough faith in spiritual things to *speak them forth* with any authority to actually *manifest* onto this material plane. We will still be dependent on the world. Our health is a matter of FAITH! Our health is a matter of authority. We must take authority, dust off our faith, and apply the Blood to the healing of our body. The power of the Blood must be *activated*. How many of us have *consciously used* the blood of Jesus in the healing of our body?! Ointment will never do any good if it is left in the tube. It must be applied! It must be appropriated to the area in need of healing if it is to do any good.

Let us begin to use our imagination and begin to 'see' spiritual realities. Let us begin to vision! Let us begin to 'see' the blood of Jesus flowing from the Cross into the cells of our body. Let us see it as a crimson river of spiritual power washing away sins, germs, and infections…purifying each individual cell… "That the life also of Jesus might be made manifest in our mortal flesh" (II Cor. 4: II). Let us see these cells being cleansed and washed of all worldly debris. "Thank you, Father that the Blood of Jesus is flowing through my body washing, cleansing, and purifying every cell in the purity of holiness. Every cell of my body is now cleansed of all sin and impurities…shining forth the Light of Christ in perfect health!"

"Christ is now being magnified in my body" …in all His glory! (Phil. 1: 20).

Let us begin to take god's view of our body! Since we were saved, God tells us that our body is now the 'TEMPLE of the

Holy Spirit" ...His property! Let us begin to think differently about our body and see it as the TEMPLE OF GOD. When our mind takes a more holy and spiritual concept as to the nature of our body, everything in our body will begin to *harmonize* in a *more spiritual* way. Heretofore, we have watched all the coughs, aches, and pains of the body on television, and run out to buy every new medicine the drug companies are promoting. They have convinced us that our bodies are sickly...and the person coughing with the flu on TV seems to send germs flying right into our living room. Next thing we know, we are waking up the next morning with some of the same symptoms! Our body just doesn't get any respect!

It is time we begin to see our body as HOLY unto the Lord...God's *Holy* Temple! It is time we take care of our body...for it is *God's property*. It is time we love it, care for it, and protect it from all the contaminations of the world. God will not have His property *defiled* forever! We have so *identified* with our *body* we think that it belongs to us...and we can do anything we want with it. God says: "Know ye not that your bodies are the members of Christ's body" ... "Know ye not that your body is the *temple* of the Holy Ghost, which is *in* you, which ye have of God, and ye are *not your own?* For ye are bought with a price therefore *glorify God in your body*, and in your spirit, which are God's" (I Cor. 6). We all have been guilty of sitting down to watch junk on television stuffing our body-temple with junk food—a great big bowl of it!

Is this really glorifying God in our body? As Christians, we cannot say that God hasn't warned us: "If any man defile the temple of God, him shall God *destroy*; for the temple of God is *holy*, which temple *ye are*" (I Cor. 3: 17). God will give us a little 'rope' to see what we are going to do with this life...and how we are going to treat our (His) body...but He will not stay His judgment forever! When we are hit with some deadly disease we will still cry out, "Why me?"

Most of us have not deliberately and consciously tried to defile our bodies, but subconsciously the ego is very much in control and still enjoys the pleasures of life...as harmful as they might be. Even though we have asked Jesus to be Lord of our lives (which should include Lord of our body) we still find the old 'self' lording it over our lives and enjoying the old habits, lusts, and personal gratifications. It is time we ask ourselves: Is Jesus *really* Lord of our lives? Do we consider our body *holy*...the *temple* of the Holy Spirit? Do we love our body and care for it as *God's property?* Do we appropriate the blood of Jesus as a healing balm to our lives...soul, mind, and body? Do we cover our body with the Blood as our divine protection and covering…insulating it from all disease and harm? How well do we answer these questions? It is time we reevaluate the way we care and look at our body. Do we really consider God's property as holy and respect it in all reverence? The body will only realize divine health when we heal the *whole* man. The body will never realize *spiritual* well-being if the soul and the mind remain sick! Soul, mind, and body must interact…working and harmonizing as *one unit*. Jesus always referred to the whole man. The medical profession, for the most part, has isolated and separated the body from the whole man. It treats only the bodily symptom. It sees only the physical. Most of us won't admit it, but many of us look at sickness more through medical eyes than through the *Word*.

We must believe the Word, see the *spiritual*, and realize the WHOLE man! It is amazing how carnal man sees almost everything opposite from God! God even says: "My thoughts are not your thoughts, neither are your ways my ways"(Isaiah 55: 8). The 'flesh' and spirit are enmity one with the other. We must begin to see the whole man…applying the Blood to every area of our body, soul, and mind. Only the Blood applied to the whole man will cleanse and bring the whole man into divine *alignment* and into that spiritual dimension of divine *harmony*.

The God-given health of the body can only be realized when the whole man is *united spiritually!*

We must begin to apply the Blood to our MIND. The mind is the housekeeper of the body. If the mind is steeped in sin and carnal thinking it will certainly be a poor keeper of the body! Let us now begin to activate our faith, through our visioning power, and begin to *appropriate* the Blood to our mind. Our imagination can be a wonderful aid in bringing our faith into a more three-dimensional, technicolor, and tangible form. Even so, it still must be *spoken* into existence by the use of God's creative words. Let us see into the creative power of faith and see the blood of Jesus flowing from the Cross filling, washing, cleansing, and sanctifying our mind in the purity of holiness. Let us see it flowing, as a mighty river, into the deep crevices of the mind cleansing and washing all memories, and subconscious thought-patterns with the Word of God. Only the washing of the Word, by the Blood, can make our old, self-centered and perverted thoughts holy and pure. Let us see the Blood lining up *all thoughts* to the Word *of God.*

Let us begin *consciously* to fill our minds with the light of the Word...with whatsoever is lovely, Godly, and of good report. Let us begin to realize our minds, too, as God's property: the MIND OF CHRIST! Let the Word bring us into that glorious, spiritual dimension of *direct knowing!* Heretofore, our mind bad been the rational mind of the intellect...fed by the five senses...a mixed bag of thoughts. Let us now see the Spirit of God *illuminating* our mind with *His thoughts!* Let us keep in mind that Jesus *only* spoke God's *Words* and only thought *God's thoughts!* He was always in the Will of His Father. He only did what He saw the Father doing. Jesus never thought a carnal thought and never spoke an idle word! So must we. It will take the training of our spirit and a real focusing of our Will...but it can be done.

Let us see the blood of Jesus flowing from the Cross into our SOUL. Let us see it as a crimson, cleansing river washing away all the left over dross of the old man...cleansing our soul of all that is carnal...purifying our soul in the Word. Let us see it bathing our emotions in the peace and joy of God's indwelling Presence—dispelling all negative emotions...all anger, all hate, all envy, all pride, etc. Let us see our soul beginning to fill up with Light...driving out all the long, dark shadows of the world. Let us see our soul now magnifying the glory of the Lord! Let our soul now open as a beautiful flowering petal...opening as a *clear channel* for the *flow of the Spirit* flowing out into manifest expression. Let the Word now saturate our soul...keeping our free-will always on course.

Let us see the Blood flowing into every cell of our body-temple…washing, cleansing, and purifying each cell in the transparency of *holiness*, Let us see each cell beginning to radiate the Light of Christ's indwelling Presence…shining forth divine health. Let us see every cell and every organ harmonizing in the radiance of God's original creation…perfect and whole. Let us see the Blood nourishing every cell in the Word…lining up the atoms of each cell in the rhythms of God's creative Presence. Jesus' life is now manifesting in every cell and organ harmonizing the entire body in wholeness! The blood of Jesus is now flowing through mind, soul, and body bringing the whole man into *spiritual unity*. Every cell of the body, every thought of the mind, and every feeling of the soul *lines up* as a channel and expression of God's Life. The washing of the Blood raises the soul, mind, and body into the higher altitudes of the Spirit…harmonizing the whole man in divine health.

The Blood is the Life. It is the life of the spirit, the light of the mind, the joy of the soul, and the health of the body! The Blood is precious. It has been spilled out…the crimson river of healing…for you and for me. It is ours…but we must appropriate it.

PRAYER AFFIRMATION
for the
APPLYING OF THE BLOOD

"Heavenly Father, I ask you to release the power of the blood of Jesus into every cell of my body-temple. This crimson tide is flowing like a mighty, cleansing river, and washing away all germs, infections, viruses, and diseases from every cell of my body. Jesus 'Himself took my infirmities and bore my sicknesses'...and 'with His stripes I am healed'! Jesus' Blood is now sanctifying and healing every cell...in divine health. The Blood in now purifying each individual cell in *spiritual holiness*. The Light of Christ is now shining forth from the center of every cell...filling my entire body-temple with Light. Christ is magnified in my flesh...radiating the glory of God's indwelling Presence! Every cell is bathing in Jesus' precious blood singing forth His praises...every cell vibrating one to the other in the divine harmony of perfect health.

The blood of Jesus is flowing from the Cross of Calvary into every thought of my MIND. My mind is now being washed of all carnal and worldly debris...every thought sanctified in the purity of holiness. The Blood illumines my mind in radiant Light...filling my mind with the wisdom and thoughts of God. The Blood is now flowing into the deep caverns of my subconscious washing away all memory-patterns of envy, lust, sorrow, hate, pride, and all the dark shadows lingering from the old, carnal self. I have the MIND OF CHRIST…my thoughts are illumined in a state of direct KNOWING! My spirit is open and receptive to the inflowing of the Holy Spirit filling my mind with the Light of God's most holy thoughts.

The blood of Christ is flowing into my SOUL. My soul is now being washed in the blood…the cleansing of holiness.

The blood is now washing away all dark shadows…freeing my soul of all fear, anxiety, sorrow, torment…all the rotting fruits of the old life. My soul is now filled with the light of God's glorious Presence. My soul magnifies the Lord! My soul is now singing forth feelings of peace, joy, and love…ever praising the Lord of my creation.

The Blood is flowing through my entire being harmonizing my spirit, soul, mind, and body in one complete unit of Wholeness…every part spiritualized in divine health."

Remember, these Affirmations must be read daily and aloud over and over and over that the Word reach down into the spirit…for full manifestation onto the physical plane.

XIII

AND THERE WAS LIGHT

The apostle John describes Jesus, the "Word made flesh", as the life and light of man. "In the beginning was the Word and the Word was with God, and the *Word was God*. All things were made by him; and without him was not any thing made that was made. *In him* was life; and the life was the *light of men*. That was the true Light, which lighteth every man that cometh into the world." Jesus couldn't have made it more clear when he said: *"I am the light of the world"*! For us to fully understand how to appropriate the Word of power for victorious living we must come to understand the oneness of the Word and Light. Jesus is the living Word. Jesus is the Life eternal. Jesus is the Light. Truly, Jesus Is! Jesus, the Word, was with God in the very beginning speaking forth the Word of Creation: "Let there be." When God's Spirit began to move He sent forth His Word into the great void of darkness and decreed Light: "And God said, Let there be LIGHT." The scriptures tell us that "That which doth make manifest is Light". Light is the foundation structure for all manifest creation. From the vibration of Light comes forth the electrons and protons of the atom. As the atoms gather together in one place they form the physical phenomenon—the molecule. Molecules, in turn, unite in units making up the cell. We see manifest creation bursting forth in consciousness as cells unite in forming the physics of our material world…manifest creation appearing through our senses on the screen of consciousness. Light is the fundamental element of all creation…Light projecting forth the radiant energy of our atomic world of matter. All is LIGHT. Our senses cannot 'see' Light, but they do pick up the vibrations emanating from Light. Our senses live on a very narrow plane of vibratory frequency…grasping only the outer surface, and projecting the 'form' as pictures onto the screen of the mind as conscious awareness. God's Spirit moved. God spoke the Word…and formed Light. If we could see our 'world' as pure Light, we could begin to live in a whole new dimension…seeing the oneness and totality of all creation. Truly, we are "complete in Him" for *He is* the "Light of the World". He is the very source of all manifest life. Once we can begin to grasp and comprehend the reality of our physical world as pure Light, the more we will understand the reality of this life in which we live. God's Kingdom is the Realm of Light manifesting forth all physical phenomena. Jesus' express purpose was to show us the Reality of life…making Himself the open door to God's eternal

Kingdom. Every believer has the opportunity and privilege to live in God's Kingdom now and for *all eternity.*

Unfortunately, most believers are waiting for eternal life after they die, and continue this present life walking the dusty road of materialism.

When we are born-again we receive Christ, who is eternal life, into our lives. Our spirit, dead in sin, has been made alive by the Spirit of God. Every believer should be radiating the Light of God's glory! Our spirit has been reborn by the power of God's Holy Spirit, and can now fellowship with God's Spirit...spirit to spirit. Yes, it is through our born-again spirit that we can enter the spiritual realm of God's eternal Kingdom. How many carnal Christians totally miss the Kingdom in this life...never really entering in. Jesus said, that the Kingdom is "nigh you" ... "at hand" ...NOW! Most believers have been so programmed to living materialistic lives through their senses that they still keep their spirits subordinate. The spirit of the believer should always be in a position of *dominance*. We are spirit-beings made in the 'image and likeness of God', and should be living from our *spirits*. God's spiritual world, His Kingdom, is a whole new *dimension*...a dimension the senses of the carnal man cannot grasp. God will allow the believer to continue to live on the material plane of sense perception, if he so desires…allowing him to reap many of the rotting fruits of disease, poverty, and turmoil…same as the unbeliever. The believer should, however, be living in the realm *of the Spirit* through his born-again spirit—God's Kingdom! God's Kingdom of Light is pure and holy. No disease can exist in the Light of God's Presence. God's Kingdom *is* His PRESENCE!

God appropriated the Word to form His Creation, and it is for us, as believers, to appropriate the same Word to the forming of our own personal world—in Christ. Contained within the Word is the Light of life. The believer must raise himself out of the bleak world of sensuality into the high dimensions of the Spirit…where all is LIGHT. We must learn to affirm the Word and *appropriate* it to *every area* of our lives. We must learn to discipline our lives in the Word. We must live, move, and have our being in the Light of God's Word and begin to grow spiritually…rising in ever higher dimensions of the Spirit! Eye hath not seen nor ear heard the glorious things God hath prepared for them that rise up into the higher realms of His Spirit…enjoying the Kingdom where all is contained. Jesus walked this earth but He was always *in* the *Kingdom!* He said he was *in* the world but not *of* it. He always lived from his spirit in the spiritual reality of God's Kingdom. He never left his Father's side. God has prepared His Kingdom for our born-again spirits.

Jesus told his disciples that he had chosen them *out* of *this world*. Our material world is a world of sense reception…and sense deception…a world of passing images. This material world is a world of illusory sense-pictures ruled by the conditioned ego. The senses have us living solely on the outer surface of form…never really grasping reality and the spiritual essence of life.

We enter God's Kingdom of spiritual reality through the portals of our born-anew spirit—and enter the Light of a whole new dimension. This is the realm of holiness. This is the realm of God's Presence. This is the realm in which every believer should be living! Jesus has chosen us out of this world. Why are we still following the world in the day to day carnality of sensual living? Why do we still grope in this world of sin, sickness, and darkness when we should be living in the Light of His indwelling Presence! We are the temple of the Holy Spirit. Christ lives within US. Yes, we have the Light of life living on the inside of us…his name is Jesus.

Let us now learn to appropriate the Word of Life and begin to *release* the Light of Christ throughout every area of our lives: spirit, soul, mind, and body. Let us learn to appropriate the Word to manifest the Light in every area of our souls, in every thought of our minds, and in every cell of our bodies. Every compartment of our souls should magnify the glory of the Lord. Our minds should be continually illumined with the Light of His Omniscience. Our bodies should radiate His indwelling Presence in divine health…every cell purified by the blood of Jesus in pure holiness.

We should be magnifying the Lord of Glory every minute of the day…always radiating forth the Light of His glorious Presence for all to see. Yes, our personal world should ever be reflecting God's beautiful Kingdom. Let us walk in the Light as He is in the Light!

XIV

BY HIS STRIPES YE ARE HEALED

God's New Covenant, sealed with the blood of Jesus, contains *everything* we will ever need for this earthly life. God's Covenant of Health is the Covenant of *perfect health. God does not establish a Covenant of imperfection. God is the Creator…the.God of perfection!* Any 'imperfection' we might experience would be our own failure in not living up to God's contract. God's perfection is built in. God's perfection is His own spiritual nature of *holiness. From the center of God's holiness shines forth the Light of His perfection. Yes, we must be holy, as He is holy.* Our *perfect* health is found in the light of His *perfect holiness!*

Let us read, study, and meditate God's holy Word…for it *establishes the Covenant*. God has etched it in stone, penned it with His own hand in our Bible, and written it in our heart. It is our responsibility to know *what is ours* in this, God's personal contract to us. It is our responsibility to honor this Covenant by *acting on it!*

The basic foundation in whatever area we are dealing with must be the *Word of* God. We must search out whatever God has promised us in that particular area that is included in our salvation. We must know what He has already made provision for before we can properly appropriate the Spirit's power—as we claim what is *rightfully ours* in Christ Jesus. When it comes to the healing and well-being of our bodies God says in third John: "Beloved, I wish above all things that thou mayest prosper and be in health, even as thy *soul* prospereth-." God wants us to be well! The health of our soul is directly related to the health of our *body*. It is all provided for in His Covenant to His children. In Psalms 107:20 the Word sings forth: "He sent His WORD, and *healed* them, and delivered them from their destructions—" How were they healed? Through appropriating the power of the Word! But are all diseases provided for in God's redeeming plan of salvation? Even cancers? If we still have any doubts God clears that up quickly in the 103rd Psalm: "Who forgiveth all thine iniquities; who healeth ALL THY DISEASES".

Christ paid an agonizing death on Calvary for our salvation—and our health. Should we not take hold of that which He died to give us? Isaiah prophesied, hundreds of years before the time of the Messiah, what Jesus would bear for us that we might be well:

"But He was wounded for our transgressions, He was-bruised for our iniquities; the chastisement of our peace was *upon* Him; *and with His stripes* (the lashes on His back) we *ARE healed.*"

Isaiah does not say that we can be or might be or will be—he says we *ARE healed!!* God open our eyes that we might see 'in the spirit', and know all that we have *in Christ!*

Once we are straight with the Word then we are ready to appropriate the power! "God sent His WORD, and HEALED them." As believers, born-again into God's family, we have WITHIN us the *power* of the Holy Spirit. It is God's Word that sets off our FAITH to *release* this mighty power of the Spirit. Appropriating the power to a specific area is like aiming a rifle. If we intend to hit anything, we must have a target. As we release this power to heal, let us keep in mind that our bodies are God's *holy* sanctuary—indwelt by the Holy Spirit. Let us keep in mind that *light* is the basic structure of the body—that God's all-inclusive Presence is the light pervading 'every atom and cell of every organ and part of our body. The darkness of disease disappears in the presence of this penetrating Light! I would suggest looking 'through' the diseased organ with our spiritual 'x-ray' eyes and 'see' it as atoms and cells filled with the glorious Light of Christ. The proper view and image-making faculty of the mind can be a most important tool in the appropriation of this power. 'See' this great healing power as a mighty rushing *river of light* flowing through every atom and cell of the diseased organ. 'See' the blood of Jesus, in its crimson color, flowing from Calvary's cross into every cell of your body purifying and sanctifying them making them 'alive' with radiant, glowing health. 'See' Jesus, in all His strength and robust health, living His life in and through you!

I have written out what I call Prayer-Affirmations for the use of appropriating this power into your body or to the person you are ministering to. The more you read these the better! Let these healing, living, restoring words sink deep into the subconscious. Read them over and over and over and over again day after day after day after day until you begin to see the *manifestation* of *Christ's life* and *health* break through! Let these 'living words' sink deep enough until they get down into your *spirit* and begin to germinate! Project the Spirit's power, like a *laser beam* into the heart of every atom and cell of your body. Keep on projecting this spiritual light into your body through these *living words* until your whole body is filled *with LIGHT*. Try to always see your body, God's holy sanctuary, filled with the light of God's Presence. Remember, disease can only live in darkness. When the Light is fully turned on in every room in your body— filling every cell with the glory and life of God—there will be no more darkness. The stress of dis-ease will flee before the *Light* of God's holy Presence…simply evaporate! Let us now begin to reclaim all that Satan has stolen from us! Let us now fill our body-temple with the glory of God's Presence.

Remember, we, as Christians, should be well and not sick to begin with. We have the *life of Christ* living in us! Show it! Let us resist the devil, fully realize who we are and what we have *in Christ*, and not get sick by *maintaining our health*.

These following Prayer-Affirmations are for *maintaining health*. Remember, there is no distance in the spirit and there is no distance in prayer. Read these aloud by inserting your own name or the name of the person you are praying for if they are not present. Read these with *authority* for you are *implanting* the Word.

Now appropriate the power!

Prayer-Affirmation
MAINTAINING HEALTH

"Father, let every atom and cell of my body—which is the temple of your Holy Spirit—be quickened by the power of your Spirit this day. Let every fiber of my being unite in reverence to your name! Fill every cell, nerve, and organ of my being with the radiant Light of Christ—and let every atom of my body sing and glorify your holy name.

Jesus, live your life in and through me—saturate every atom and cell of my being with your Presence.

Holy Spirit, flow like a mighty river through my body with your Healing Power and bring your freedom and health to every cell of my body. Let my physical body be now Spiritualized and be one with the Glorified Body of Christ."

PRAYER-AFFIRMATION
for
DIVINE HEALTH

Jesus is my health…my life…my all in all. My body is God's temple…the temple of the Holy Spirit. God created my body in His image, likeness…and perfection. He created my body perfect in every detail.

Christ hath redeemed me from the curse of sickness. He, himself, took my infirmities and bore my sickness… "by His stripes I AM healed—"

"Whatsoever doth make manifest…is LIGHT". My body radiates the Light of God's PRESENCE in *perfect health*. My body is filled with LIGHT. Christ is magnified in every atom, cell, and organ of my body-temple.

The indwelling power of the Holy Spirit is now being released from the center of every cell of my body…quickening every organ with the resurrection power of the living Christ.

Christ: Our Health

The blood of Jesus is now being released in every cell cleansing, washing, purifying and sanctifying every cell and organ in Divine Health. The blood is now washing away all germs and infectious diseases from the systems of my body. My body is pure, holy, and undefiled. My body is PURE SPIRIT and rejects all pollutions that would infect my body-temple. The blood of Jesus covers and insulates my body from all worldly sin and disease. Every cell is saturated with the blood of Jesus and is sin-free. Every germ that comes near God's holy temple dies instantly, in the name of Jesus.

The power of the Holy Spirit is now flowing through my body-temple. The healing river of the Holy Spirit is now rushing through my central nervous system…washing away all congestion that would cause blockage in my brain and spinal cord. These nerves are now FREE… "for whom the Son has set free, is free indeed."

Nerve impulses now flow freely through my central nervous system…every nerve filled with the Light of God's PRESENCE…God's Light is now dissolving all obstructions. My body functions perfectly in the Light and Glory of God's all-inclusive PRESENCE. "By Jesus stripes I AM HEALED" …and I claim only DIVINE HEALTH for my body, in Jesus' name.

THE CELL LIFE

My body-temple is God's master composition of cell life. Every cell of my body vibrates its life in perfect harmony to God's indwelling Presence. Every cell of my body shines forth the light of Christ manifesting perfect health in every fiber and organ. Every cell of my body is continually being charged with the atomic forces of God's Presence—regulating every bodily function in divine harmony. The health of every organ of my body is the reflection of the light of His Presence in EVERY CELL! The blood of Jesus continually cleanses and nourishes every cell with divine health. The Holy Spirit flows as a mighty river through every cell charging every organ of my body with the power and life of Christ. My body-temple is continually bathed and saturated with God's Presence vibrating every cell with His love-song of life and light. Every cell of my body is aglow with His love…every fiber of my being radiates His divine Presence. All is health. All is light.

All is GOD!

APPROPRIATING THE BLOOD

Heavenly Father, I ask you to release the power of the blood of Jesus into every cell of my body-temple. Wash every cell in the purity of Jesus' blood…let every cell, fiber, and organ be sanctified and cleansed in divine holiness. Release the power of the blood to sanctify every nerve cell…that my nerves rest in the peace and harmony of your indwelling Presence. Release the power of the blood to sanctify every cell of my heart and lungs in the purity of divine health. Release the power of the blood to sanctify the chemistry of my body in pure holiness…let every gland of my body rest in the glory of your Presence in all perfection. Release the power of the blood to sanctify every atom, cell, and fiber of my brain…let my brain function in perfection and holiness…radiating the Light of Christ.

Let this crimson tide, flowing from the cross of Calvary, wash away all disease, in harmony, congestion, and all darkness from every organ of my body-temple. Father, I thank you for the cleansing power of Jesus' precious blood bathing every fiber and organ—releasing the Light of your Presence from the center of every cell. In the Light of your Presence shines forth the strength and health of every cell…every organ magnifying your glory in divine health.

Let the sanctifying power of the blood raise the vibration rate of every atom and cell to the high vibrations of your Spirit. Spiritualize every cell of my being in the radiance of your Presence—in PERFECT HEALTH.

XV

WALKING IN THE SPIRIT

"That the righteousness of the Law might be fulfilled in us, who walk not after the flesh, but *after the Spirit*"

Rms. 8: 4

God's eternal Law of the universe is the Spiritual Law of pure holiness. The *fulfillment* of God's Law is found *in* Christ...for Christ is the spiritual embodiment of God's unconditional love-nature of absolute *purity*. Yes, there is a *spiritual dimension* to life we cannot begin to comprehend with the eyes of the flesh...and, yet, it is possible to walk *into this dimension* by our daily 'walking in the Spirit'. John tells us to "walk in the Light, as He is in the Light." This Light-dimension of the Spiritual Realm is a reality of life far beyond the limitations and plagues of this sensual world. God tells us to be *holy*, for He is holy. There is absolute purity to holiness. The contaminations of this world would be instantly filtered out as one enters the great and awesome Presence of God's holiness. A beautiful Biblical example of a man that walked in this dimension of God's most holy Presence is found in the fifth chapter of Genesis. Here it is recorded: "And Enoch, walked *with* God: and he was not; for God took him." What a beautiful example of "walking in the Spirit" …walking so close to God that he did not even see death! Enoch actually walked in a dimension that transcended death! Yes, God is Light…a glory Light which no darkness can penetrate. "For ye were sometimes darkness, but now are *Light in the Lord*: walk as *children of Light*" (Eph. 5-8). Enoch was born into a world of darkness, but, as he daily walked with God, walked right through the veil of darkness *into the Light* of God's glorious Presence! "Let us walk in the Light of the Lord" (Isaiah 2: 5).

God tells us in Exodus 29: 42, 43 that He will *meet with us* and *talk with* us at the door of the tabernacle. "And there I will meet with the children of Israel, and the tabernacle shall be *sanctified by my glory*". Under God's New Covenant our body has become God's tabernacle…the Temple of the Holy Spirit. This *holy* temple has been *sanctified by the blood of Jesus*. This tabernacle has been cleansed from the sins and contaminations of the world…this tabernacle of our body is *holy* unto the Lord. God's glory has come in! Enoch must have reached a point in his walk with God that he was continually *embraced by the Glory!* He walked right into the Glory dimension…the dimension of Light. This dimension transcends the earthly shadows of disease and death. Enoch did not die of disease in a struggle against death. Enoch walked with God right out of the jaws of death…right into the glory dimension of God's most holy Presence! "God is Light, and in him is no darkness at all" (I John 1: 5).

"In the beginning was the Word, and the Word was with God, and *the Word was* God. All things were made by Him; and without Him was not any thing made that was made. *In Him* was Life; and the Life was the *light of* men. That was the true Light, which *lighteth every man* that cometh into the world. He was in the world, and the *world was made by Him*, and the world knew Him not. But as many as received Him, to them gave He *power* to become the *Sons of* God"(John 1). Jesus, the author of Life, was the eternal Word that spoke forth the whole of Creation. Jesus, the eternal Word, is the Life and Light of man. He was the universal Light that "Lighteth every man" that came into this world…and all that come to Him will He give the power to become the "sons of God". God's children are the "children of Light". These are those that have the *Light of* Life dwelling within them…His name is Jesus. These are those whose robes are spotless white…washed in the blood of the Lamb.

It was the Word, in the beginning with God, creating the Worlds…created in the *substance of Spirit…manifesting* through the vehicle of *Light*. Light is the foundation structure of this material plane. Light is the power base of this atomic universe. The atomic radiation of Light structures the molecules of our cellular world. The cell is the common denominator of all plant, mineral, and animal life. The cellular life of our body is composed of the atoms of Light. We live in a world of Light, whether we know it or not.

This is the dimension of pure Spirit...pure holiness. This is the manifest Presence of God's glory. No disease, no plague, no darkness, no evil can live in the Light of God's Omnipresence. This is where Enoch walked and talked with God. This was the dimension where, on the Mount of Transfiguration, God opened the eyes of Peter, James, and John, and they saw into this glorious *dimension of Light and beheld Jesus in His glorified body. They saw, for a brief moment, into God's World of Reality!*

How important it is for us, who are born-again by the blood of Jesus, to *walk with* God and enter into this same intimate relationship as Enoch. Most believers, sadly to say, are walking more with the world than with God. They have become so mesmerized to the world of the senses that they are hardly aware of God's Presence within. They have bought into the ways and methods of the world. They identify more with the world than with Christ living on the inside of them. Even with the Light of

Life living on the inside, they still walk in the dark shadows of sensual living. They are not keeping themselves 'under the blood'…and find themselves susceptible to every germ, every disease, every evil…same as all unbelievers of the unsaved world!…All because they have failed to walk in the Spirit…walking with God—into the Light of His glorious Kingdom! God is Love. Walking through this life 'in the Spirit' is not only an intimate relationship with the Father, but is the 'walk of Love'. We must walk in the very nature of the Father…which is Love. We not only have the inner relationship of a deep and intimate fellowship with God, but the *outer* expression of *God's love* to hurting humanity. Yes, we are known by our love. This is unconditional, Agape Love…a love that only *gives out God's love-life*. Divine Love. This is such an intimate union with the Father that only His Love shines through our lives. It is the *releasing* of this inner fountain of Love that magnifies the glory of the Lord as a beacon of Light to a world of darkness. We become the *channel* for the flow of God's Love-life. This is not a walk of human effort, but the walk of the Holy Spirit. The Holy Spirit has been given free reign in our lives to release His mighty power…the miracle-working power of Love!

Our life now becomes one of praise and worship. We find ourselves releasing all that we are and have to the Father. We have become lights in a world of darkness. "That ye may be blameless and harmless, the sons of God, without rebuke, in the midst of a crooked and perverse nation, among whom ye *shine as lights* in the world; Holding forth the Word of Life." (Phil. 2-15, 16). We have *purified* ourselves in sinless living, through the washing of the blood, and have become a *clear channel* through which God might work: "For it is God which *worketh in you* both to will and to do of His good pleasure" (Phil. 2: 13). We wake up with God *at work* doing *His will* in our lives, and projecting His will through our lives. We go to bed at night resting in His bosom. We can only praise Him!

Our health can only be a byproduct of His glorious Presence within. This is not something we have to 'work' at. Christ is alive in us. His life in us *is* our health! No demons of sickness dare come near the holiness of Christ!

It is "no longer I that liveth, but Christ living *in me*". My entire identity has been dissolved into the Christ-life. His life has been so *activated* within me that His love-life radiates through every cell of my body-temple…shining forth perfect health. We can only praise Him!. He is the "Light of Life". He is the Word of Life…the Word that not only created the worlds in the beginning...but is *ever* creating. Yes, creation is an *ongoing act!* He is the Author and the Life. "There is but one God, the Father, *of whom are all things*, and we *in Him*; and one Lord, Jesus Christ, *by whom are all things*, and we *by Him*" (I Cor. 8: 6).

Our health is a gift...the gift of Grace. It is established in God's New Covenant for His children...children who walk hand in hand with Him...ever walking in the Spirit. "Every good gift and every perfect gift is from *above* and cometh down from the *Father of lights*, with whom is no variableness, neither shadow of turning" (James 1: 17). We must come into our *new identity* in Christ, *ever aware* of *His life* in *us*. The Light of His life in us is the glory of the soul, the illumination of the mind, the radiance of the cell, and the life of the spirit. Our health is *built in*. This is perfect health.

Christ is our health, our life, our all in all! Let us daily 'walk in the Spirit'...activating the life and power of Christ within us as the very reality of our life.

XVI

PRAISE: GOD'S PRESCRIPTION FOR HEALTH AND HEALING

"I shall yet praise Him, who is the health of my countenance, and my God"

(Psm. 43: 5)

Christ paid for our salvation with His own precious blood upon the cross of Calvary…God's ultimate and final sacrifice. He died to set us free from sin's dark bondage. He died to present us to His Father…redeemed for all eternity. His blood sealed the New Covenant of Grace. His resurrected life resurrected the doomed soul of man, and marked the beginning of time…birthing God's Covenant of Grace for all eternity. Man's soul began to breathe in God's eternal life, and the sun began to dawn upon a bright, new and glorious day. His blood bought salvation for all those who come to the foot of the Cross. Christ's blood-bought salvation is all-inclusive…lacking in nothing…the Life "more abundant." Truly, we are "complete in Him" (Col. 2:10). His salvation includes *everything* we will ever need in this present life including our health! "By His stripes we are healed"! How few of us have really come into the full realization of so great a salvation! Christ did not die to give us an imperfect, incomplete, or lacking salvation. He died that we might have His life…in all its love, purity, and fullness.

How can we let so great a salvation go unfulfilled…never fully incorporating it into the fabric of our lives? How is it that the spiritual life Christ planted within us, in the person of the Holy Spirit, is still earthbound? We are still following all the same old, dusty paths of the world! Did not Jesus tell His followers that He had chosen them "out" of *this world?* Do not the scriptures tell us to forsake the world and be "transformed" as *new creations* in Christ? The fullness of our salvation can only be realized in its totality as we "abide *in* Christ, and His *words abide in us—"* Jesus said that though He was temporarily *in* this world…He was NOT *of* it.

The Christ-life that we, as believers, should be living is a totally *new dimension!* This is a dimension far above this sick and poverty-stricken world. Only the Christ-dimension contains our glorious salvation in *all its fullness*. This is a dimension far above poverty, sickness, and all the plagues of the Curse that darken this planet. The carnal life of mere 'existence living' can never rise into this glorious dimension…for it is eternally burdened down with a dead spirit. God, open the eyes of your church that it no longer neglects so great a salvation! How we continue to crucify Christ anew by refusing to accept the finished work of our salvation in *all its fullness!* How can we honestly say we are 'saved' and continue in the carnality and mind-set of the world?!

Let us no longer neglect so great a salvation and rise up in the Spirit into the *Christ-dimension* where all is light, love, peace…and health! It is time we no longer grieve the Spirit of God by giving so little value to the Blood of our Redeemer. We are the REDEEMED! The Blood of the Lamb of God has brought us all, as brothers and sisters in Christ, into the family of God. If we are truly living and abiding *in* Christ, with His Word abiding, germinating, and growing in us, we will begin to rise up into this dimension where our salvation is fully realized as a completed reality…far above all sickness. His life in us will truly be a well-spring of living water ever bubbling up from our innermost being…ever lifting us in higher dimensions of the Spirit. The church has not even begun to realize the infinite dimensions and spiritual realities of the Christ-life! The fullness of our salvation is all-inclusive. It is finished…complete in every detail: Yes, we are "*complete in Him*": spirit, soul, and body.

The Holy Spirit was given to each believer as the *inner power* to live the Christ-life in total victory over every circumstance. The fullness of our salvation will only come, as a reality in this earthly life, in proportion to our *living in* Christ. Jesus said, "Ye must be born again." He did not give us a brand new, born again spirit just to continue to live in the carnality and filth of this sin-infested world. We became born again with the express purpose of ABIDING IN HIM! Jesus said: "*If* ye abide *in me*" …ask what ye will…and you shall receive my great salvation in *all its completeness!* Every promise of God is conditional…*IF*. God tells us we can only receive salvation and eternal life *IF* we receive Christ as our savior. God says we will only know the completeness and fullness of our salvation *IF* we abide in Him. God says we will only know His perfect health (included in our salvation) *IF* His words abide in us: "By Jesus' stripes I *am* healed." Yes, it is all ours…*IF!*

We will never *have* that which we do not *know* is ours! We must search the Bible, and find all of God's promises to His children, to fully know *all* that our salvation includes. Because of the supreme sacrifice of Calvary God has deposited the totality of salvation in our own, personal banking account. If we do not know we already have it in the bank…we will never make a withdrawal! We must claim it! It is all *ours* in the bank of heaven! Jesus has paid the price. Let us not neglect so great a salvation!

Christ: Our Health

God is a FAITH-God. Without faith it is impossible to please Him. Our senses have totally mesmerized us to this material world. The 'world of the senses' is like a giant movie screen…ever hypnotizing us to this world of matter. We sit before this giant screen (in consciousness) totally spellbound. We cannot seem to escape—for sensual stimuli bombards our mind our every waking hour. It takes the 'force of faith' to blast us through this material hypnosis into the spiritual realities of God's Kingdom. God's glorious Kingdom can only be entered through the Cross of Calvary…on wings of our born again SPIRIT. Our natural eyes will never see into the realm of the Spirit. Our natural mind will never know the great mysteries of God. Our natural ears will never hear the voice of God. Nevertheless, there is a dimension to life that few of us have ever experienced. It took *faith* to receive our salvation, and it will take *faith* to *receive all* that salvation includes!

God tells us in His Word to be "not *conformed* to this world"—but to be "*transformed* by the renewing of our mind." Our mind is not automatically 'renewed' the moment we are saved. This renewal is a process…the process of *spiritual growth*. Our mind is renewed through the WORD…reading, study, meditation,…and, literally, speaking God's Word over our lives. The Word of God must become more real to us than this 'world of sense perception' we are submerged in. The Word will bring light into our consciousness, and we will soon find ourselves being *transformed*... "until Christ be *formed* in you" (Gal. 4: 19). If we do not intimately know the Word of Life we will never *know what is ours in Christ*. As we come into the knowledge of Christ we will begin to undergo The Transformation revealing God's Presence filling all in all.

When we enter this door of Knowledge knowing who we are in Christ...we can only praise Him. We enter the courts of God's glorious Kingdom with songs of praise. As we behold this new world of infinite beauty...filled with His glory...we can only praise and worship Him. "Thou art holy, O thou that *inhabits the praises* of Israel" (Psm. 23: 3). How close we draw to God when we praise Him...for He *inhabits* our praises! As we praise Him in sickness we will feel His Presence welling up within us and magnifying His Life and Health in every fiber of our being! We can only worship and thank Him for so great a salvation!

Whenever we begin to sink in the quicksands of materialism, in utter despair, let us remember that God "INHABITS the *praises* of His people" ...and praise our way right back into His PRESENCE where *we belong!* How easy it is to slip back into the mindset of the world. Before we know it we're thinking like the world, talking like the world…and walking with the world. Jesus told us to be *separate*…that His Kingdom was "not of this world" …to keep ourselves separated from the sins and carnality of the world. We are to be HOLY…as He is holy! It will take the purity and transparency of holiness to live *continually* in this *spiritual dimension* of God's most holy Presence. PRAISE is the spirit-wings that will keep us high and lifted up…high above all the sickness of this world…high above all the bondage and limitations of the flesh.

Remember when Paul and Silas were in prison bound in chains? At the midnight hour Paul and Silas prayed and sang praises to God. God heard their prayers and praises of worship and sent a great earthquake to loose their bands and opened the prison doors! Surely, God does *inhabit* the praises of His people! Praise is our surest and quickest way out of bondage…even the bondage of sickness. Praise energizes the Spirit. Praise lifts the Spirit to the place of dominance. Praise releases spiritual power in the infrastructure of the cell-life. Praise shines the light of Christ as the glory of the soul; the Illumination of the mind; and the health of the body. "Then shall thy light break forth as the morning, and thine health shall *spring forth speedily*: and thy righteousness shall go before thee; and the glory of the Lord shall be thy reward" (Isa. 58: 8). When this 'light of health' is turned on, by flipping the switch of praise, we can say with Paul: "Christ shall be MAGNIFIED in *my body!*" (Phil. I-20). When the Light of Christ is being fully magnified in the cell-life of our body all shadows, symptoms, and appearance of dis-ease will VANISH! All the sick spirits of darkness will flee before the glory-light of God's most holy Presence!

Jesus said that if we failed to praise Him, the very stones would cry out in praise. God gives us this beautiful description of our body: "Know ye not that your body is the TEMPLE of the Holy Spirit which is *in* you, which ye have of God, and ye are *not your* own? For ye are bought with a price: therefore *glorify God in your body*, and in your spirit, which are God's" (I Cor. 6: 19, 20). Yes, our body is God's property...His holy temple...the housing of the Holy Spirit! Every cell must sing His praises! There is no such thing as 'dead' matter. God created every atom and cell of this universe from the substance of His *Omnipresent Spirit.* "One God and Father of all; who is above all, and *through* all, and *in you all*" (Eph. 4.-6). God's very life is the spiritual substance of all matter...including the cell-life of our body-temple! God's Omniscience is the supreme Intelligence of every cell.

God's Omnipotence is the very atomic energy releasing in every cell. Let every cell of our body praise Him—for God *inhabits* the praises of His people. God will release His quickening power within each and every cell as they begin to respond to our voice of praise and worship. When we praise Him and thank Him for so great a salvation, His omniscience in every cell will surely respond...releasing the power of His Omnipotence! When this power is released—*health* is released. The quickening power of praise restores every sick and damaged cell to the high vibration of health and wholeness! Let every cell praise His holy name!!

When Satan places a symptom of sickness upon our physical body we must immediately resist it by praising God for His divine health...thanking Him that our body is the Temple of the Holy Spirit...and quoting God's words of health. We must never be denied our total package of salvation! We must defeat the devil with Christ's words of authority: "It is written."

It is written:

Praise God – "Christ hath redeemed me from the curse of sickness"

Praise God – "By Jesus' stripes I AM healed!"

Praise God – "Jesus took my infirmities and bore my sicknesses"

Praise God – "The blood of Jesus cleanses me…making me whiter than snow"

Praise God – "Christ is magnified in every atom and cell of my mortal flesh"

Praise God – "The Blood of Jesus covers me…protecting me…healing me: spirit, soul, mind, and body"

Praise God – "Every cell of my body is sin-free…sanctified in holiness and righteousness unto the Lord"

Praise God – "Every cell of my body praises Him for His great salvation"

Praise God – "Every cell and every organ sings His praises…my body-temple is filled with the Light of His Presence"

Praise God – "For Divine Health in Christ Jesus!"

Doctor's write out expensive prescriptions for every known disease, but God's prescription is *free*! Praise is God's heavenly prescription—ever lifting us higher—lifting us into the spiritual dimension of God's most holy Presence…far above all sickness! Let us not neglect 'so great a salvation' through ignorance, neglect, and compromise! How we have grieved the soul of God! Life is a matter of choices as we encounter its many tests and trials. How often we find ourselves in the deep, dark

Christ: Our Health

pit...the "trial of our faith". How often we find ourselves in the black dungeon of sickness with not so much as a ray of light. Satan has tipped the scales of life and we find ourselves in the depths of despair and pain. How easy it is to complain, moan, groan, and give up...further tipping the scales to Satan's advantage. God tells us to PRAISE him in *all things!* Let us follow Paul's and Silas' example and praise ourselves out of the dungeon. Let us praise ourselves through life's many trials...tipping the scales back to the God-side of life and health.

Our spirit must be in total *dominion* over every facet of life. It is the power of praise that lifts the spirit to its rightful place of dominance. Our born-again spirit must be in total control...always in control of the mind and body. Praise is God's prescription for health. Praise is God's cure. Praise heals! Praise brings the light of God's glorious Presence right into the heart of every sick cell. Praise releases the resurrection power of the Holy Spirit to the restoration of wholeness and health to every cell. Every sick cell responds to the quickening power of God's Spirit...as we praise Him. Praise energizes every cell to the high vibration of divine health. Let us praise Him! Let us praise Him for a salvation that is lacking in nothing. We are "*complete in* Him". "Christ bath *redeemed* us from the curse". He bath redeemed us from every curse of Deuteronomy 28.

Christ did not go back to the Father saying it is "finished"…just to leave us with an incomplete salvation. Praise is the thankful voice for all He has done for us…ever thanking Him that He has given us EVERYTHING in our salvation!

Praise God…from whom all blessings flow! Our mind must praise Him with beautiful thoughts. Our soul must praise Him magnifying His glory. Every cell of our body must praise Him. Every fiber and organ of our body must praise Him for His holy Presence lighting every cell. Let everything that hath breath PRAISE THE LORD!

Praise ye the Lord!

XVII

CHRIST: OUR HEALTH

"Christ shall be magnified in my body"

(Phil. 1: 20).

When Christ is fully magnified in our body, then our body can only *manifest health! Christ is our* health…when *fully manifesting!* Jesus made it perfectly clear when He said that we should abide in *Him* just as *He abides in us*. Christianity is: "Christ-in-me". Christianity is the gospel…the 'good news' of Oneness. "I am the vine, ye are the branches: He that *abideth in me*, and I *in him*, the same bringeth forth much fruit: for without me ye can do nothing…If ye abide in me, and *my words* abide *in you*, ye shall ask what ye will, and it shall be done unto you." Jesus summed it all up when He prayed this final prayer to His Father: "That they all may be one; as thou, Father, art in me, and I in thee, that they also may be *one* in us…I in them, and thou in me, that they may be made *perfect* in one—" The gospel of oneness is the gospel of the all-inclusive Christ.

Yes, the Christ of Eternity is *everywhere present*: the great "I AM". God is Omnipresent, and the Light of Christ manifests the whole of Creation…in, above, and through all things. We bear in our body the limitations of life due to our *limited definition* of Christ. We have failed to incorporate His allness into the fabric of our own lives. We pray to Him, we seek Him, we believe on Him. This is fine (and has become the foundation of our Christian faith)…yet, He still remains on the *outside*. Instead of looking without we should be *releasing* His life *from within*. Jesus is still knocking…waiting to come *in*. Jesus said that we are to "eat of His flesh, and drink of His blood" …to fully *consume* all that He is. He must become flesh *of our flesh!*

We certainly became a "new creation" when we were saved…making Jesus lord and savior of our lives. But, with many Christians, who have failed to grow spiritually, the Christ of our salvation seems to be more or less dormant as the *Reality* of our lives. Often it is difficult to distinguish the saved from the unsaved outside the church walls. Many believers remain carnal Christians…living the same materialistic lives that they lived before they were saved.

God is certainly pleased to see that we are saved, but, I'm sure, very distressed to see Christ in us ignored. Christ cannot assume His *lordship* of our lives if He remains asleep!

If we look closely, we will still see the ego on the throne…and very much in control. Jesus will not share His lordship…He, alone, must rule. He can never be Lord if we just let Him sleep, barely even recognizing His *indwelling Presence*. How can He fulfill His mission *in us* if we do not so much as acknowledge His Presence in us? Christ will never be more to us than we allow *Him to be!*

How many of us, as believers, still cling to the old life. How we still enjoy the pleasures, the desires, and the accolades of the old man. We have been *resurrected* with Christ…a totally *new* Creation! The old man that was crucified at Calvary, should have been left in the grave. How many of us, deep down, want it both ways. We want the freedom and joy of the new life…but we want all the sensual pleasures of the old life, too. We are still attempting to resurrect the old life. When we were saved, the former body of sin should have been buried…once and for all! Christ must now be to us *everything*…our all in all! We are not recycled, patched-over creations…we are an entirely *new* creation! Christ is everything…but His allness will only manifest experientially in our lives in *proportion* to our *recognition* and *living His Presence* within.

We are "complete in Him" …as long as His Presence is *fully manifesting* in our lives! He longs to live His Life in and through us. He longs to be *everything* we will ever need. He is *in* the lives of all believers…but still *asleep* in most! It is our responsibility, as Christians, to awaken Him, and release His dynamic power to *every area* of our lives! The Light of Christ must be released to spirit, soul, and body! "When Christ, *who is our life*, shall *appear* (in full manifestation), then shall ye also appear with Him in glory" (Col. 3: 4).

Yes, His glory will be our glory…when fully manifesting in our life!

Our health is *in Christ*. When we are fully incorporated in Christ *nothing else exists*. "Christ is all, and in all". He is the great Reality…pure, perfect, and holy. He is the Light of all Creation. "In him was life; and the life was the *light of* men—" If we could but see life from a different perspective, and view the world from the center of the cell, we could lose the prejudices, and associations that have so influenced the way we see things. The cell has a life of its own. The individual cells compose larger organisms. The health of each cell is its ability to transmit light. The health of the body is directly proportionate to the light-transmission of each cell.

Christ's Presence, in the believer, whether he is aware of it or not, is the sum and substance of his existence. "By him all things consist—" Yes, He *is* all in all. "For we are members of His body, of His flesh, and of His bones." Just as we, collectively, (the church) are *in* Him, like individual cells of Christ's body, so, too, is He *in us*—the *substance* of each individual cell. As we abide in Him, so *He abides in us*. As we have been incorporated into His life, as the body of Christ, so has He become incorporated into our life…flesh of our flesh each cell radiating His glory. "The *light of the body* is the eye: therefore when thine eye is *single*, thy *whole body* also is *full of light*. If thy whole body therefore be full of light, having *no part* dark, the whole shall be full of *light*." Here, in a nutshell, is Jesus' prescription for the health of the body. Here is God's Law of health. Either Christ is magnified in the body, manifesting as Light, or He is not…and the separation of darkness continues to prevail. A cell, void of light, exists in the shadow of death…darkness.

When we are saved, we receive Christ into our heart.. our spirit is resurrected by the power of the Holy Spirit…and our soul is redeemed unto the Father—saved for all eternity. But, the body awaits its glorified state. The body can still be sick and subject to the law of death. This does not mean that the death of the body must come as a result of the body ravaged by disease—like the unbeliever. The *believer's* body *should be* well…filled with the life and light of Christ! Death should be a simple smooth transition into the glories of Eternal Life.

Jesus said that the only way the glorious Light of His Presence could reach the cell-structure of the body was through the "single eye". Only the 'eye of the Spirit' totally *focused* on

Christ, could emit light into the cell-composition of the body. This is the only way the body can become "full of light"! For Christ to be magnified in our body each cell must, individually, *take on His life*. Each cell must be resurrected...the *spiritualization* of the body! Each cell must begin to transmit the Light of Christ. Each cell has a life of its own.

The spiritualization of the cell-life will never rise above the *spiritualization of the* mind. The mind is the 'housekeeper' of the body. Our mind must be singularly *focused on Christ*. We must rise up out of the carnal mind into the 'mind of the spirit'. Certainly, this can only be a "mind stayed on Thee". The 'eye' of our spirit must be singularly focused to transmit light as a *pure channel*. It is possible for Light to flow from the realm of the Spirit into and onto the physical plane of the cell-life. The pure *holiness* of the *spiritual* mind can affect the pure *health* of the body. This is what Jesus meant by the 'single eye'. Most all believers carry with them, to some degree, the dark-ness of the carnal mind. We, as Christians, must become totally *spiritually minded*, "For they that are after the flesh do mind the things of the flesh; but they that are after the Spirit the things of the Spirit. For to be *carnally minded* is death; but to be *spiritually minded* is life" ...that "Christ be magnified in our *body*"!

Christ: Our Health

Christ is not only our healer...Christ *is* our health! Jesus was the "Word made flesh". Now that we, as believers, have received Him into our lives He must now become the very essence of our being...even flesh of our flesh! Jesus, the "living Word", must come alive even in the "flesh" of our body. God tells us that our body is now the *temple* of the Holy Spirit. Our body is His 'holy temple! Only in the light of *pure holiness* can the body begin to manifest the allness and glory of God's Presence! Only health can exist in the Light of God's Presence! The disease of each cell is simply a cell void of light. Yes, the darkness of sin's curse still casts its shadow upon the cell-life...slowing the vibratory frequency of the cell into the cycles of death. But, the good news is, we are no longer subject to the bondage of death...*if* the eye be totally single! It is only the singular 'eye of the spirit' that can channel God's Spirit onto the material plane of physical manifestation.

God's glory does not need to be limited. It is possible that Christ can even be magnified on the physical plane of the body. "But if the Spirit of Him that raised Jesus from the dead dwell in you, He that raised up Christ from the dead shall also *quicken your mortal bodies by His Spirit* that dwelleth in you—"

"For if ye live after the flesh, ye shall die.-but if ye *through the Spirit* do mortify the deeds of the *body, ye shall live*. For as many are led by the Spirit of God, they are the Sons of God." Paul is addressing this to the *body*, and not to the soul. He is addressing this to believers whose soul is already saved...even though they still possess, to a larger or lesser degree, the carnal mind. Everyone seems to be living "after the flesh" to some extent...leaving the body subject to the 'law of death'. Paul is reminding the believers at Rome that the Spirit of God now dwells within them...and that their bodies have been transformed into God's holy temple. He reminds them that there is "now no condemnation to them which are in Christ Jesus, who walk not after the flesh, but after the *Spirit*. For the law of the Spirit of life in Christ Jesus hath made me free from the law of sin and death".

When the eye is totally *single toward Christ*...then the body can fill up with *Light*. Let us now begin to walk *in the Spirit* into the full *Light of His Presence*...and begin to realize Christ as OUR HEALTH!

ABOUT THE AUTHOR

Author, cellist, and artist Dan Lynch has devoted much of his life in the search for Truth…a search for the reality of life underlying the façade of this 'material' world of sense perception. He realized early in his life that much of the problems and sickness people face in life are the consequences of ignorance.

As a cellist he has played in major orchestras, performed in Carnegie Hall, owned a Stradivarius cello, and studied with Pablo Casals. As an artist, he has shown his paintings at galleries throughout the country, owned his own gallery in Carmel, and is creating the artwork for church bulletins. As an author he has written hundreds of poems, and nine Christian books. His poems are currently being printed by Blue Mountain Arts.

Ten years ago the Holy Spirit, out of the blue, inspired Dan's first book. This was, more than likely, the overflow of a lifetime of searching for THE ANSWER to sickness in his family. The Lord tested his faith and resolve to find the answer…an answer that only God could answer.

Christ: Our Health is the revelation of the spiritual dimension to health and wholeness according to God's Word.

Printed in the United States
701500003B